Happy New Year!

and Other Stories

DOVER · THRIFT · EDITIONS

Happy New Year!

and Other Stories

SHOLOM ALEICHEM

Translated and Edited by
Curt Leviant

DOVER PUBLICATIONS, INC.
Mineola, New York

DOVER THRIFT EDITIONS

GENERAL EDITOR: PAUL NEGRI
EDITOR OF THIS VOLUME: CURT LEVIANT

DEDICATION

For my friends
Lester and Ethel Segal

Bibliographical Note

Happy New Year! and Other Stories, first published in 2000, is a new selection of eleven unabridged stories reprinted from *Stories and Satires* by Sholom Aleichem, translated by Curt Leviant, and originally published by Thomas Yoseloff, New York, in 1959. A new Introduction, written by translator Curt Leviant, has been specially prepared for the present edition.

Library of Congress Cataloging-in-Publication Data

Sholom Aleichem, 1859–1916.
 [Selections. English. 2000]
 Happy New Year! and other stories / Sholom Aleichem ; translated by Curt Leviant.
  p. cm. — (Dover thrift editions)
 "Selection of eleven unabridged stories reprinted from Stories and satires by Sholom Aleichem."
 ISBN 0-486-41419-1 (pbk.)
  1. Sholom Aleichem, 1859–1916—Translations into English. I. Leviant, Curt. II. Title. III. Series.

PJ5129.R2 A25 2000
839'.133—dc21

00-031777

Manufactured in the United States of America
Dover Publications, Inc., 31 East 2nd Street, Mineola, N.Y. 11501

Introduction

By NOW THE facts of Sholom Aleichem's life hardly need elaboration. Born in a shtetl in Russia's Ukraine in 1859, Sholom Aleichem (his real family name was Rabinowitz) was the first Yiddish writer to combine the age-old oral Jewish/Yiddish humor, anecdotes, and short Hasidic tales with the Western esthetic/literary tradition. From about 1890 on he was one of the major figures in modern Yiddish literature, and along with his mentor, Mendele Mocher Seforim (1836–1917), and I. L. Peretz (1851–1915), was one of its founding fathers.

For the next 25 years he was considered one of the living legends and culture heroes of Yiddish-speaking Jews all over the world. When he died in New York City in 1916—two years after emigrating to America in 1914—more than 150,000 Jews accompanied him to his final resting place. So unique was the event, so enormous the outpouring of love and respect for their beloved humorist, that the *New York Times* gave the funeral a page-one story. And so enmeshed in the psyche of Jews is the life and death of Sholom Aleichem that, a few years ago, at the conclusion of a lecture I gave on the writer, an elderly woman shyly came up to me and said in Yiddish, with a measure of pride, "Do you know, I was only a youngster then, but I attended Sholom Aleichem's funeral!"

From the standard 28-volume Yiddish works of Sholom Aleichem, three major figures emerge who live in and near his mythical Jewish shtetl, Kasrilevke: Tevye the Dairyman who sells milk, cheese, and sour cream; his relative, Menachem Mendel, the poor unemployed luftmentch who roams away from home trying to scrape up a living; and Mottel the Cantor's son, the epitome of Jewish childhood, who soon leaves for America in an actual and symbolic shift of the center of gravity of Jewish life from Eastern Europe to the United States.

It should be noted that these three characters are not purely comic creations. Like the Jewish people, they have their doses of anguish.

Tevye's life is actually suffused with tragedy; yet the mere mention of his name to a Yiddish- or even English-speaking Jewish audience suffices to elicit a smile. This is because Tevye's speech is peppered with humor, irony, and optimism even as he describes the sad events surrounding his daughters, his wife, and his own forced exile from the village in which he spent most of his life. The same may be said of the hapless Menachem Mendel, and even Mottel, where in one famous scene, he exclaims, "Hooray, I'm an orphan!"

The edgy laughter-through-tears mode that Sholom Aleichem mastered often contains more tears than laughter. With pogroms and increased anti-Semitism, he witnessed a decline of Jewish life in his homeland. Had he lived twenty more years beyond his relatively young 57 years, he would have witnessed the beginnings of a total decimation of European Jewry: the rise of Nazism in Germany which would ultimately take the lives of six million European and Eastern European Jews, and the tightening noose of Stalin's Russian anti-Semitism, which choked the spirit of Russian Jews, its Judaism, Hebrew learning, and tradition. (At least under the Czars, despite censorship, Hebrew and Yiddish literature thrived.)

In this collection, we see another major hero—the fourth—this time an unnamed first-person narrator who represents the average, small-town Jew in his habits, quirks, humor, attitudes, and peregrinations. In the monologue "Geese" we meet the woman who sells geese and tells about it in a kind of Yiddish stream of consciousness. In digressions she lets us know about several people in town whom she dislikes, always apologizing with a repeated tag-line, "You know what they say: a woman was made with nine measures of talk."

This monologue, along with "Three Calendars," "Happy New Year," "At the Doctor's," "Three Widows," "On America," and "75,000" are superb fictions that show how closely Sholom Aleichem was linked with his contemporary, the great Russian short story writer, dramatist, and creator of monologues, Anton Chekhov (1860–1904), whom Sholom Aleichem knew and admired and who, alas, also died at a young age of tuberculosis.

This collection contains several other first-person stories—"Passover Eve Vagabonds," "The Ruined Passover," and "From the Riviera." ("Someone to Envy" is the only traditional third-person narrative in the book.) However, they are not monologues, for they lack the tight focus of a one-person telling, contain longer dialogue exchanges, and, above all, lack the device of the narrator talking directly to the invisible listener, who is occasionally reminded of the I-you link—mostly on a train where both teller and listener are captive between stations (even though the train locale is not always revealed).

Many of the stories here, like "Three Calendars," are comic masterpieces. Darker tales, like "Three Widows," one of Sholom Aleichem's unrecognized brilliant achievements, are not often critically discussed, but they reveal another aspect of the writer's genius. And the modernistic touch of the absurd, which occasionally surfaces in his writing (seen here in the hilarious "On America," in the person of the great bluffer Berl-Ayzik), shows Sholom Aleichem approaching 20th-century modernism head-on.

CURT LEVIANT

Contents

GEESE

I DON'T WISH this on anyone, but a year ago *Hanuka* time, I had a stroke of good and bad luck at one and the same time. Just listen to this story! You run across a gem like this only once in a thousand years. I've been selling geese, you see, and kosher-for-Passover goose-fat for these past twenty years, and in all that time, a thing like that's never happened to me.

Geese is my business . . . but you think it's as easy as all that? The first thing you got to do is this: you start buying geese right after *Sukkoth*, in the autumn. You throw them into a coop and keep them there all winter, until December. You feed them and take good care of them. Comes *Hanuka*, you start killing them, and you turn geese into cash. If you think it's so easy to buy them, feed them, kill them, and turn them into cash, you're wrong. First of all—buying the geese. You have to have something to buy them with! And I don't have any reserve money salted away, you know. So I'm forced to go and take a loan from Reb Alter. You know him, don't you? He enjoys squeezing the blood out of you, drop by drop. That is, he doesn't say no right off the bat. But, with his telling you to come tomorrow, the next day, the day after that, he drives you to the breaking point. Then he gets down to work, dragging the interest out of you, adding on extra days. He's some Reb Alter! It's not for nothing he's got such a pot belly and his wife's got a face I wouldn't wish on my enemies and a pair of jowls you could sharpen knives on. Talk of her pearls! Just recently, she had an engagement party for her daughter. Great God! May you and I have a third of what that party cost her. Then I wouldn't have to bother with geese any more. But you ought to see the fellow she got! May God strike me if I'd take the likes of him for *my* daughter. First of all, he was as bald as an egg. But, anyway, the whole affair is none of my business. I don't like to talk ill of anyone, God forbid, and I like to stay away from backbiting. I'm getting off the track. I'm sorry, but that's a habit of mine. You know what they say: a woman was made with nine measures of talk.

1

Buying geese. . . . Where do you buy them? You'd think, at the marketplace, naturally! Surely! If we'd be able to buy all our geese at the marketplace, we'd be rolling in gold. If you want to buy geese for business, you have to put yourself out and get up early, at an hour when God himself is still asleep, and traipse way over to the other side of town, behind the mill. But there you'll find another woman, just as smart as you, who's gotten up earlier and made her way over to the same spot. Then there's a third one who got up earlier than both of you—and that's the way it goes. The whole thing turns into a fishmarket. Everyone stands around waiting, hoping that God'll have some pity and send along a peasant with some geese. And as soon as he shows up, the women close in on him and his birds.

"How much for a goose?" they yell.

If the peasant is the sort of businessman you can talk to, why then you can bargain with him. But if, with the help of God, he's a nervous wreck, you can't even come near him.

"Beat it," he says. "Scat. I don't have any geese."

Well, what can you do. Sue him? You can only mumble, half in Yiddish, half in Russian. "How so, you hick peasant? We see with our own eyes—may your eyes ooze out—that you're carrying a goose—may devils and plagues carry you to blazes."

And he says: "I don't have any geese for sale."

But, if God is merciful and the peasant has let go of the goose, then you have to inspect it. And you have to know how to inspect it, too. People say that you have to be as much a connoisseur of geese as of diamonds. You probably think all geese are alike. Do you happen to know that there's such a thing as a goose and a gander? And that a goose *isn't* a gander. A goose'll give fat, a gander—plagues! But how can you tell the difference between them? Easy. First of all, by the comb. A gander has a little comb on the top of his head and a long neck. You can also tell by his voice. He has a gruff voice, just like a man. When he walks, he always struts ahead of the geese. Forgive the comparison—just like a man. Our husbands—it makes no difference who they are, even the worst bunglers among them—always walk ahead of their wives, as if to say: "Lookee here! It's me!" Need more proof? Take my husband, for instance. There's no greater bungler than my Nachman-Ber. Ever since I've known him, he hasn't earned two broken kopeks. Then what's he good for? He's a scholar and a distant relative of a very rich man. His granduncle's second cousin twice removed! But what do I get out of that? May my enemies choke on it in one bite! Trouble, heartache, and shame is what I get out of it. This rich relative's daughter-in-law doesn't wear a marriage-wig, so they throw it up to me. Can you beat that? And it's no lie either! They hit the nail right on the head! But I don't want to gossip about her or talk behind her back. I'm getting sidetracked. Sorry, but that's the way I am. You know what they say: a woman was made with nine measures of talk.

Buying geese. . . . Once you've bought them you put them into the coop for the winter. If you think that's an easy job, you're sadly mistaken. It's easy to coop them up if you've got a private apartment. But what're you supposed to do if—and I hope it never happens to me or you or any other Jew—you're sharing a place with Yente: that is, if you don't have a little room you can call your own and your landlady, who's called Yente, is also selling geese and kosher-for-Passover goose-fat. Well, I'd like to see you try and keep your geese and her geese in one room and not come to blows three times a day. That's the first thing. Next, try and be the smarty and tell which geese are your geese and which geese are her geese. Listen to what happened some time ago. And I don't wish this on anyone. I was sitting in the room when, suddenly, the door of her coop flew open and her whole pack of geese ran out and made a bee-line for my sacks of oat- and barley-feed. Who do you think suffered? Who was supposed to raise a storm? Me or her? Don't you think she let *me* have it?

"If I would have known," she said, "that you *too* keep geese," she said, "I'd never have rented you this room," she said, "for a hundred million rubles."

"What'd you think was my business," I told her, "selling jewelry?"

"You're a jewel yourself and you got yourself a gem of a husband and diamonds for kids."

Expect me to take that sitting down? She's a queer one, that Yente! Usually, she'll do anything in the world for you. If you're sick, God forbid, she'll drop everything just to take care of you. But she's a hot-head. You really have to watch out for her. One *Hanuka*—wait, just listen to this story and your hair will stand on end. The only trouble is that I don't go poking my nose into other people's business. I don't like to gossip or talk behind other people's backs . . . But I've lost the thread of the story. You'll have to forgive me, that's the way I am. You know what they say: a woman was made with nine measures of talk.

Let's continue. Putting the geese away. . . . If you want the geese to grow good and fat you have to put them into the coop just before the beginning of the month. Don't you dare come near any geese just *after* the new moon! May God save you from misfortune like that. The geese will be ruined. Their bones will be heavy, their skin scraggly. Don't expect any fat at all! Just forget about it. Don't cage them during the day either, when everyone is around. It's much better toward evening, with candlelight, or better yet, in complete darkness. And when you do do it, pinch yourself and say three times: "I hope you get as fat as me." My husband makes fun of me and says that my hocus-pocus isn't worth a snap. If I'd listen to everything he says, I'd be in some pickle. All he does is sit and study, day and night. I'll never understand why he likes to say that twirling a chicken around your head on the eve of *Yom Kippur* is a silly custom. How do you like that for nerve? Don't worry, he didn't get off lightly for that, either.

"Did you come to that grand conclusion all by your little self?"

"That's what the books say," he says.

"Then the upshot is," I say, "that I and my mother and Aunt Dvorah, and Nekhama-Breyne, Sosi, Dvosi, Tsipora, and all the rest of us are a bunch of asses!"

My genius doesn't answer, and he can thank his lucky stars he doesn't, because I'd let him have it so that his ears would be ringing for three days in a row. But don't think, God forbid, that I'm such a shrew and spitfire. Believe me, I know how to respect a man of learning, a man who sits and studies Torah, despite the fact that he doesn't so much as put his finger into cold water. You think he's lazy? He'd do anything, poor fellow—but there's nothing to do. So he sits and studies. Let him keep studying. Why should he work if I can take care of everything myself? I can manage, if not to cover expenses, then at least not to go begging. I do everything by myself. Shop, keep house, cook, put up the potatoes, dress the kids, and what's most important—send them off to Hebrew school. As you can see, there's bread in the house—but sometimes there's no white-loaf for the Sabbath. But although stones fall from heaven, there must always be money for the kids' Hebrew lessons. I got four boys, you see, may they live and be well, not counting the girls. I'm not like these modern folk who push their kids to gentile schools. Take Berel the Cantor's boy, for instance. He's become a complete heathen, sausages and all, the devil take him. But after all, I'm not God's lawyer. I'm not doing any backbiting, God forbid, and I can't stand the evil tongue. . . . There I go, mixing one story with the next. I can't help it; that's one of my bad habits. You know what they say: a woman was made with nine measures of talk.

You've put the geese away. . . . Now, you just have to see to it that the geese get their feed and water in time. That's all there is to it. For geese aren't ducks and chickens, you know. Ducks are scared of the pox. Chickens of polecats. But geese just glut. When it comes to eating, anything goes. Oats, millet, groats, and, begging your pardon, they peck at worse things, too. A goose isn't choosy. Everything goes down the hatch. A goose is always hungry, just like—and no comparison meant—a poor man's children. A poor man's children eat anything you give them with gusto. And they're never full. I know it from experience. Let them live and be well, my children, God bless 'em, come home from school and—well, before you turn around, they've killed a full loaf of bread and licked a whole pot of potatoes clean. They don't even leave a crumb. Comes the Sabbath, you have to portion out the white-loaf like cake and lock up the rest; for if you don't there won't be a trace of it left by morning. But it's nice having children. It wouldn't faze me at all having ten, fifteen, even seventy-five children. There's only one drawback. They got mouths! The rich are as lucky as anything knowing that their kids go to sleep with full bellies and don't dream about beggars and don't wake up crying, "Mama, I'm hu-un-gry." You feel sorry for them, you understand, and you practically go out of your mind. Can you imagine having to tell them: "Get back to sleep, you little devils. Who's heard of eating in the middle of the night? Back to sleep!" On the other hand, you ought to see the storm the rich raise when, God forbid, an extra baby is born to them. Tsk, tsk, tsk. Just recently, one of their young mothers died. She was a fine, good-hearted, beautiful girl—the picture of health. Do you know what she died from? I'd rather not talk about it, for she's in the other world now, may she have a bright Paradise. I don't want to slander anyone, and I like to put distance between myself and the evil tongue. . . . But, you see, I'm forgetting about the story. That's the way I am, so pardon me! You know what they say: a woman was made with nine measures of talk.

Oh, me, what a business geese is! That is to say, it isn't such a bad business, and if God blesses the geese you can make a pretty ruble out of them. But what's the rub? That only happens once in ten years. More often you don't make a kopek from the geese. In fact, you end up in the red. You put so much work into the whole mess, that I swear it isn't worth the tumult. If so, you're liable to ask, if there's no profit in geese, why bother? Here's my answer—what else do you want me to do after working with geese all these years? Think of it! Tying up thirty geese, carrying them over to the slaughterer, coming home with thirty of them, plucking their feathers. Then salting, rinsing, and scalding them. Then separating the skin, the fat, the giblets, and the meat, turning everything into money, not letting a speck go to waste. And I do it all by myself. First of all, I fry the skin and the fat and make goose-fat out of it. I make Passover-fat every year, for my Passover-fat is considered the best and most kosher fat in the village. When I make kosher-for-Passover goose-fat, Passover steps into the house smack in the middle of *Hanuka*. I make the oven kosher-for-Passover. I send my husband to the synagogue. Let him study there. I chase the kids out of the house. Let them go play with their *Hanuka dredle* somewhere. Goose-fat hates extra company. Especially Passover goose-fat. Once, when I lived with Yente, I got myself into the sort of fix I wouldn't wish on anyone. There were other people living there at the time. One of the women, Genesi it was, suddenly got it into her head to start making buckwheat *latkes*. Just on the day I was killing my geese and had the house kosher-for-Passover. I begged her, "Genesi, darling, honey, sweetheart! Put off temptation just one more day. God willing, you'll make your *latkes* tomorrow."

"It's all right with me," she said, "but the children'll find out. My little gluttons enjoy eating. As soon as they find out there's no *latkes*, the little cannibals will start eating me."

She hit the nail right on the head. The little children, lying on the shelf atop the oven, heard that the *latkes* would be postponed for the next day. One of them, a little cross-eyed boy named Zelig, screamed: "Mama, if you don't make *latkes*, I'm going to throw myself off the shelf." We looked up, and oh, me! The boy was leaning over—in another minute he'd fall off and be broken to bits. Seeing a performance like this, I shouted, "Genesi, darling, honey, sweetheart! Make your *latkes*, quick!"

They say that a pauper has a bottomless stomach. That's true as the Bible. You ought to take a look at Genesi's children. May God spare me! But I'm not talking ill of anyone, God forbid. And I can't stand backbiting either. There I go—I've lost the thread of the story. Forgive me, but that's my nature. You know what they say: a woman was made with nine measures of talk.

Geese to goose-fat. . . . You can't expect goose-fat and goose-fat alone from the geese. If you do get some fat out of them, it only covers the investment. The profit comes from the left-overs. First of all, goose-meat. If the geese turn out well and the price of meat in town is high, well, then, you're the boss. But what happens when the butchers have a price war and meat is as cheap as dirt, and to top it off the town has imported a new slaughterer and the old slaughterer slanders him and says that he's one of those modern smart-alecks, a Zionist who piddles with Hebrew Schools and Zionist dues and our town's rich man doesn't think much of these Zionists anyway and says that they're a bunch of sots and since the new slaughterer's slaughtering isn't any good and not everyone is eager for goose-meat—what happens then?

"You can buy the goose-meat from me without thinking twice," I argue with my customers. "They're perfectly kosher. The old slaughterer killed them."

"You're absolutely right," they say, "but the point is there's no tag on them saying who killed them. It could be *anyone*."

"What do you mean there's no tag?" I say. "If I tell you the old slaughterer killed them, the old slaughterer killed them. On the other hand, it's a sad state of affairs if it's come to the point where you don't trust me."

"You're a queer one," they say. "We trust you to a *t*. But if we can have our own geese sent to the old slaughterer ourselves, why do we have to buy *your* goose-meat, if we don't know who the slaughterer was!"

"Blast it," I say, "you're starting from scratch again. They're kosher! I swear it by the life of my husband and children. And you know that that's a good oath."

"Why swear?" they say, "we believe you anyway."

"Then why don't you take a few pieces of goose-meat off my hands and lighten my load?"

"We can't take them because we don't know who slaughtered the geese."

Well, go talk to the wall! Try to put yourself into someone else's shoes—that, they'll never do. Have some pity! A woman breaks her neck over the geese, hoping that she'll make a little something out of it. We had some winter! There was no wood and straw was so high you had to pay a ruble for each wagon-load. The poor children went to school barefoot. They came home blue with cold and clambered up on top of the oven and snuggled in like little rabbits, waiting for hot potatoes, and you couldn't buy potatoes with gold. Part of the crop failed, and part of it rotted underground. What a town! You'd think someone would care. Poor people were dying of cold, they were swelling up with hunger. The children were falling like flies. But it wasn't so terrible, because only the poor were dying. May God not punish me. I'm not talking ill of anyone. I don't want to gossip. But, I seem to have lost the thread of the story. Sorry—but that's a bad habit of mine. You know what they say: a woman was made with nine measures of talk.

Goose-meat. You'd be in some pickle if you only depended on the goose-meat. Besides that, there were fried scraps and livers and gizzards and heads and feet. Then there were gullets and wings and tongues and hearts and kidneys. Not to mention necks. There's one woman I know who buys up every single neck I have. Even if there's four dozen, she takes them all. It's her husband, she says. He goes wild for necks and white meat. He eats the white meat cold and peppered. He prefers the necks stuffed either with flour and groats, or with chopped liver and crisp *grieven*. And it makes no difference to him if it's roasted separately or cooked with carrots. Well, what do you say to that? Like the saying goes: the dead look the way they eat! And you ought to see that woman's husband! Compared to my husband, he looks like a man of thirty, God bless him, although he's a good ten years older than my Nakhman-Ber. Although my husband doesn't do a stitch of work besides poring over his books, when he comes home, he doesn't grunt like other men and say: "Listen here, bring some food!" The first thing he does when he comes home from the study room in the synagogue, is pick up a book. He reads it and sighs quietly. That means he's hungry. But he'll never say it out loud. What, then? He groans, puts his hand to his heart, and says, "Oh, me." That shows he's really starving! "Want something to eat?" I ask him. "All right," he says. No matter how much I tell him, "I don't understand you. You got a mouth, why don't you use it? Why do you have to sit there and moan?"—it does no good. Go speak to the wall. I'd like to see what would happen if, on purpose, I didn't feed him for three days. But do you think he's got *that* many bees in his bonnet? How can a scholar like him be such a ninny? If with what he knows, he'd just be a little more of a pusher, don't you think he could be the village rabbi? But, then, what would we do with our old rabbi? Come to think of it—what are we going to do with our old cantor? We just got a new one, you know. We needed him like a hole in the head. We got him so that the old cantor could starve because— after all—he wasn't much of a pauper beforehand, anyway. Why'd all this come about? Because the village rich man likes good singing. You want to hear good voices? Go to the theater and they'll sing you to death there. If I were only a man I'd show them a thing or two. Boy, would I take care of them! Do you think I have any squabbles with them? Nah. I just hate their guts. I can't stand those rich big-shots. Spiders and rich men! May God not punish me. I'm not belittling a soul, and I don't like to criticize anyone behind his back. But I'm getting off the track. Well, that's the way I am, you'll have to excuse me. You know what they say: a woman has nine measures of talk in her.

Well, what you get out of the geese. . . . Don't think that you're in clover once you've sold the goose-fat, all the meat, and the giblets. If geese didn't have feathers and down, the whole business wouldn't be worth its weight in salt. When I start, that is before I even put them into their coops, I feel them under the armpits, and scrape away the little bit of down I find there. There's even more after they're killed. Then I take the feathers and the down separately, and prepare work for the whole winter. The nights are plenty long and there's time enough for plucking. So I sit and pluck. I have a little help, too. My girls. Girls aren't boys, you know. Boys go to school. But what do girls do? Girls are like a bunch of geese; they sit at home, eat, and wait to grow up. I sit them down in front of a sieve and tell them to start plucking feathers. "If you do," I say, "tomorrow, God willing, I'll smear some goose-fat on a piece of bread and give it to you. Better yet, I'll make a soup out of gizzards." You should see them rush to work. It's nothing to sneeze at—a soup made out of gizzards. What can I do? We don't even see a piece of meat all week long, not counting the Sabbath. If I didn't sell geese, I don't know what I'd do with my children all week long. Like this, they manage to get hold of a little gullet, a gizzard, a head, a foot, a drop of goose-fat. The smell alone is enough for them. When I lived in Yente's house—and I don't wish this on anyone—my neighbor Genesi told me: "You know, when *Hanuka* rolls around and you start messing around with your Passover geese and kosher-for-Passover goose-fat, a new life comes into my little gang. The smell of the cooking alone makes them dizzy and they think that they're eating goose-meat."

You think it was easy to look at a mob like Genesi's, poor souls, and see them ogling the pot of goose-fat and the frying *grieven*. They didn't even so much as stick their hands out and say "give me." They just stood there and stared, like hungry wolves, licking their lips, their eyes shining. It was pitiful watching them. What can you do? You give them each a little *grieven*—you wet their lips with a bit of goose-fat. I couldn't do any more, though. How can I start feeding so many mouths if I am flooded with a brood of my own, may no harm come to them, and to top it off, have a husband who never earns a wooden kopek and we haven't even paid for the geese yet? I wish I had a third of what I owe. The interest grows like wild mushrooms and you have to pay it. I'm not going to run out on my debts and I'm not going to go bankrupt either, God forbid, like Yente did when she didn't pay her brother-in-law for the other half of the apartment because her son was a student and, as they said, wrote on the Sabbath. Anyway, that's what they say. I don't know. I wasn't there. I hate to talk about things I don't know about and I hate to run other people down. Just let me ask you one question. Why does Yente's son have to study? He's sick too, unfortunately—consumption. The whole family—and I don't wish this on anyone—is consumptive. But let her live to be a hundred and twenty. I'm her friend. What have I got against her? But on the other hand, she didn't do right by me. You don't go kicking your roommate out of the apartment just before Passover. What was the matter? Menashe the Water-carrier was able to pay the ruble-a-week rent and I wasn't. First let her get a kopek out of him, *then* let her talk. Folks say he's up to his neck in debts. He doesn't even own the hair on his head. He's gotten his money for his winter's work in advance and he's still a pauper. He's married to Peysi, and she's a vixen to boot. May God not punish me. I'm not talking ill of anyone, I hate backbiting you know. But . . . hold up . . . I think I started out to tell you a story! But for the life of me, I can't remember what it was. Women are nothing to sneeze at, you know. They're some brood. Look here. I've mixed up everything under the sun, livers and feathers and last winter's snow. You know what? A woman *was* made with nine measures of talk. I'll just have to put that story off for some other time!

THREE CALENDARS

YOU WANT TO know why a Jew like me, a father, handles contraband filth like French postcards? I've got Tolmatshov and Tolmatshov alone to thank for it, may he fry in hell! But since it all happened so long ago, and since Tolmatshov is no more, and since Odessa is back to normal, I think I can come out with the whole truth as to why Tolmatshov was such an anti-Semite. And the truth is, that I'm to blame for most of it, I'm afraid, if not all of it.

Well, now you're probably wondering how a street-hawker like me, who peddles Yiddish newspapers and French postcards on the sly, comes to General Tolmatshov! And what sort of friend am I with generals, anyway? But the answer is, you understand, that every why has its wherefore, and that a Jew is only human. If you can spare a few minutes, I'll tell you an interesting story.

It happened right here in Odessa, many years ago, at this time, during the intermediary days of *Sukkoth*. Generally speaking, Odessa was still the same old Odessa. No one had heard of Tolmatshov, and a Jew could roam around as free as a bird and sell his Yiddish books. Then, there weren't as many Yiddish papers as today. You weren't afraid of anyone, and there was no need to mess around with banned Parisian postcards. In the old days, I used to sell Sabbath and holiday prayer-books and Jewish calendars around Lanjerovski, Katerinenski, and Fankonin streets. You could always run into a Jew there, for that was the area where speculators, agents, and various other Jews hung around waiting for a miracle.

Just like you see me now, I was strolling along on Fankonin Street, the spot where our speculators wear out their shoe-leather looking for business, and I said to myself: where do I get a customer for the few calendars I got left? *Rosh Hashana* and *Yom Kippur* are gone and forgotten and before you know it, *Sukkoth* will slip right by and I still haven't gotten rid of my little bit of stock. God knows if I'll ever sell those bound calendars—for it's the sort of stuff you can't even *give* away if it isn't sold before the holidays. Later, they're completely useless. And I had *three* of them left over from before the Jewish New Year!

I started off with a hundred and got rid of them on the street, mostly among the stock speculators. They weren't such fiery Jews—I mean, they didn't go for Yiddish books and all that. But when it came to a Jewish calendar for the entire year, well, even that sold. After all, you had to know when Passover or the memorial day for a loved one came. A Jew is a Jew after all.

Well, strolling about that way, I stopped near Fankonin and looked at the group of speculators running back and forth. I knew every single one of them blind-folded, and I thought: who can I offer these few calendars to if each one's got his supply? I don't think I missed a one.

As I stood there thinking, I saw a general with as many medals as I got hair, sitting at a front table at the outdoor cafe on Fankonin. He was stirring his coffee with a spoon and talking to a servant, repeating the same thing over and over again. And each time the servant answered: "I get you, Your Excellency."

What's he trying to tell him? I asked myself. I edged up closer to the general's table—I'm only human, you know—and made believe I was looking somewhere else. I heard the general slowly telling that thick-headed peasant what to do. He literally put each word into his mouth.

"Remember what I'm saying," the general said. "Go to my house, at Number 3 Hersonski Street, and tell my wife that Count Musin-Pushkin is having dinner with us. Don't forget now. Number 3 Hersonski Street! Count Musin-Pushkin!"

The servant stood at attention. His only words were: "I get you." When the peasant left, the general called to him again: "Remember, 3 Hersonski Street, Count Musin-Pushkin!" He was about to return to his coffee, when he spotted me standing there almost on top of him, gaping into his glass. Not that I meant any harm by that, God forbid. I just stood there— just like that. Well, he raised his voice and stared right through me.

"What do you want?"

What I want, you won't give me, I thought. But then again, maybe yes! So I got a bright idea. I'm only human, you know. Believe it or not, I told him: "Your Excellency, how would you like to buy a calendar?"

He looked at me. "What sort of a calendar."

"A Jewish calendar," I said.

He looked at me as if I was completely crazy and said, "What do I need a Jewish calendar for?"

"I don't know what you need it for," I said. "But I need money for the holiday. I have three left, you see. How about buying one, Your Excellency?" And I thought: it'll be some neat trick if he'd buy a Jewish calendar.

Well, here's what happened. No sooner did I say the word "Excellency," than he boomed out, "Go away, please."

Believe it or not, my blood froze. I'm only human, you know. I grabbed my bundle and was ready to about face, when suddenly I heard him say "Come back here."

What could I do? I had to go back. He asked me to show him a calendar. I did. Then he wanted to know how much it cost. I told him. He paid me for it right away without bargaining, without saying a word, without anything. How's that for a general? Isn't he worth three speculators?

Well, that's a start, I said to myself, taking my bundle and going. A start was well and good, but what next? Where do you find two other generals like that on whom you can palm off two leftover calendars. Then I got another brilliant idea! I'm only human, you know. Why not offer him a second one? No skin off his back, having two Jewish calendars. But what would he do with two? Come to think of it, what would he do with *one*? Thinking like this, a new idea hit me. I remembered how he tried to pound the address—Number 3 Hersonski Street—into that peasant's thick skull. As I lived and breathed, that was where I could find a home for a second calendar.

Now don't be a bungler, Avram Markovitsh, I said to myself (that's my name, you see), and strike while the iron is hot. Nab yourself another buyer. Then, without dilly-dallying, I crossed one street after another until I got to Hersonski Street, and looked for number 3. Sure enough, there it was! And what a number it was, too! A private, two-story brick, building. Fine and dandy, but what next? Ring the bell and ask for the general's wife. And that's just what I did, thinking—I'll be in a pretty fix if a soldier shows up, probably with a dog to boot. He'll toss me out on my ear and set the dog on me. That's all I needed!

Two minutes passed, then three. But no one showed up. What luck I have, I thought. No one's in. But, perhaps the bell's out of order. Must try again. And believe it or not, I upped and rang again. Once, twice, three times—finally, the door swung open and there stood a peasant girl, holding a broom.

"What do you want?" she said.

I wanted to run real quick, but I took my heart in my hands—I'm only human, after all—and said: "I have to see the general's wife. It's something personal."

She looked at me as if to say: what a queer bird *he* is. Then, without so much as a by-your-leave, she slammed the door in my face. What a welcome! But maybe she'd come back. Then, again, maybe she'd send the soldier and the dog, I thought, and wanted to make a quick retreat. But since I was already there and had rung the bell—it was too late.

Half a minute later, the door opened and there stood a beautiful young woman—all peaches and cream. Was she the general's wife? Couldn't be! Too young. The general's daughter? Nope. *He* was too young. But time was a-wasting.

"What is it you want?" she said.

What now? I thought. Should I address her as "Your Excellency"? If she really was the general's wife—then it would be all right. But what if she weren't? Why should I give her an honor gratis? I'm only human, you know. So I decided to eliminate the title and start from scratch.

"The general bought a calendar from me and asked me, that is, told me to deliver it to Number 3 Hersonski Street and that's where they'd pay me for it. And in case they didn't believe me, the general gave me a sign that Count Pusin-Mushkin was eating supper here tonight."

She broke into a laugh. "It's not Pusin-Mushkin—but Musin-Pushkin."

So long as you're laughing, lady, I said to myself, you're all right. "Be that as it may," I said, "Pusin-Mushkin, Mushkin-Pushkin. What's the difference? So long as the sign is right." I handed her the calendar. She took it and turned it around and around, inspecting it from all angles. "How much is it?" she asked. I told her. Then she took the calendar, paid for it, and smiled a good-bye. How's that for a lady? Pure gold! She was worth not only three speculators—she was worth three dozen! So I got rid of the bigger part of my stock. Only one was left. I could now go home and eat supper, right?

I had supper and rested, but that one calendar was bothering me. True, I'd gotten rid of two out of three—was stuck with only one. But for that very reason, I wanted to get rid of that last one, too. What good was an old bound calendar? Therefore I *had* to get rid of it. But how do you go about it, if most of the speculators already had theirs? No choice but to roam through town once more. Without dawdling, I took my bundle and went out. Just like that. Since I knew the two main streets, my feet took me there without being asked. Right to where the speculators ran around, wearing out their shoe leather. Where else was there to go? Perhaps God would soon provide a customer. After all, it was only one little old calendar. And, believe it or not, I wandered back and forth, like a lion in a cage, looking at the speculators and watching them scurry about like chickens without heads, looking for business. Everyone looked to make a ruble. But, in the meantime, while pacing around and looking toward Fankonin, I spotted another general. He too was full of medals. Here's a neat one, I thought. It's a God-send. Another general. A customer for my last calendar.

A thought flew through my head. It's a shame I didn't have any more calendars. For if generals start to buy Jewish calendars, *all* the speculators can go to hell and take the entire stockmarket with them.

While thinking, I looked and realized that it was *my* general. Believe it or not, I recognized him right away. Evidently he recognized me, too. How do I know? I saw him stand up and wave me over to him. Bad situation. What now? All I needed now was to get mixed up with generals. I kicked up my heels and started running, good and proper. I'd figured it out and knew that with such leg-work I'd put three streets between me and him in two minutes flat. That's exactly what happened. Half a minute later, I heard someone tailing after me, hollering for me to stop.

Who was it? Could it be the general himself, in all his glory? What an eager-beaver of a general! Just look what was happening! A Jew had sold an extra calendar—and what a commotion. Generals chasing me. Bad! Bad business! What was the next move? Run faster? But suppose he whistled for the cops? That's all I needed—an arrest! But if I stopped, he'd nab me with that second calendar fraud. Better to make believe that I didn't know what was happening and go my own sweet way—not running, but not crawling, either, just sort of stepping smartly, like a man busy with his own affairs. But what if he caught me and asked why I was running? Then I'd tell him that that was my way of walking.

But here's what happened. He caught up to me. Bad, huh? But listen to the upshot. Well, if you were caught, there was nothing to be done. So, I stopped and looked. But where was the general? General! What general? Baloney! It was just one of the waiters from the Fankonin cafe. He'd run with a napkin tucked under his arm, and was wiping the perspiration from his face.

"Damn you," he said to me, when we both had stopped. "Why'd you take off like a wild billy-goat? The general wants to see you?"

What general? And how do you know it's me he wants?"

"What do you mean, how do I know? Think I'm deaf? Think I didn't hear the general say: there he goes, the Jew with the books. Catch him and bring him over."

If that's the case, I thought, then all hell hasn't broken loose yet. Doom isn't at hand. I could always think of something at the last minute. I'm only human, you know. Like a flash, a brand new idea hit me. Maybe a miracle would happen and I'd get rid of my last calendar. Without batting an eyelash, I slapped my forehead in mock surprise, spat, and said:

"Well, why didn't you say so in the first place? You should have told me it's the bookish general. He's a queer one. All day long he's been bargaining with me for this book. He's run me to death. It costs a ruble and he keeps offering me a half. I've already told him 75, 70, 60 kopeks. Let's call it quits. But he's as stubborn as a mule and won't budge from that half ruble. I should drop dead right here and now that if this weren't my last book, I wouldn't let him have it for a kopek under the regular price. But since it *is* the last one, as you can see, hand over half a ruble and here—run back and give him this book."

To this day, I don't know who the general was! But my guess is that it was none other than Tolmatshov himself. If not, why did he suddenly let loose such a murderous reign of terror against Jews in general and more so, against Yiddish book-peddlers in particular? We peddlers of Yiddish books and newspapers felt his wrath more than anyone else. To this very day, we don't dare show our faces on the streets selling a Yiddish book or paper. We have to hide it inside our coats like contraband or stolen goods. May my enemies, your enemies, and all enemies of the Jews have as many good years as we have profit out of dealing with hot Yiddish papers. So, I have to have a sideline—French postcards—some loose, some sealed in envelopes. And they're my main item. I handle the newspapers just for fun. But there's a bigger turnover in Parisian picture postcards. The speculators take to them more readily than to the Yiddish papers. Oh me, I know it's a foul business and I'll have to answer for it someday. . . . But what can you do? You're only human. A Jew has to make a living—the kids want to eat. . . . God'll probably forgive me. He'll *have* to forgive me. Has he got a choice? What do you think? Here it is *Hoshana Rabba* already—and final judgments are being sealed.

May it fall on his head—the judgment, I mean. On Tolmatshov's head! For if it weren't for him, may he rot in hell, I'd still be selling prayer books and Jewish calendars instead of this filth. By the way, can I interest you in something? I just got a new shipment in fresh from Paris.

HAPPY NEW YEAR!

IMAGINE, EVERY SINGLE one of them up to Mr. Big himself takes bribes. Don't be shocked now—Mr. Big himself accepts them, too, if he gets an offer. What's that? You don't believe me? You're all laughing, eh? Well, have fun. . . . Ready now? Have you all laughed yourself dry? Now gather round me, brother Jews, and listen to a story that happened a long time ago to none other than my grandfather, may he rest in peace. It happened in the good old days when Czar Nich was boss. What are you nudging me for? Why be scared? You think these peasants sitting here know what we're jabbering about? They won't understand a word, blast them. I won't be obvious and where necessary I'll throw in some Hebrew. Just pay close attention and don't keep interrupting me and everything will be fine.

To make a long story short, it happened in the days of King Ahasuerus—in other words, during the reign of our present Mr. Big's grandfather, after whom he's named. May his grandfather have an easy time of it in the other world, for all the favors and fine and dandy things he let loose against our brethren—Amen. Our fathers and grandfathers just couldn't forget that old Mr. Big. Even when they suddenly awoke from their sleep, they thought well of him. That's how well off they were. In short, their whole life hung on a thread. We were allowed to exist just by the grace of little Mr. Big, or Buttons, as we called him. This Buttons liked to have his palms greased, and loved those Friday night snacks of *gefilte fish* and tumblers of whiskey. So long as this went on, the Jews breathed free and easy, did business, plied their trades, and really had a wonderful time.

But once—and whenever you hear *but once*, you know trouble's coming—something happened. Buttons kicked the bucket. He suddenly just upped and dropped dead and was followed by a new Buttons, a Haman, a villain, a rat, the likes of which you've never seen! He couldn't be greased; he just wouldn't take a thing! They tried slipping him bigger bribes. Still, no. They tried the real thing—big money. Still

16

nothing doing. They invited him for *gefilte fish*. He wouldn't go. They dropped hints about rare liqueurs. He didn't drink. Talk of being ethical! He was as clean as a whistle! If you begged him, he stamped his foot, kicked you out on your ear, and then did things which just weren't done. He kept issuing summonses; he slapped one fine after another on you. He didn't let Jews do business. He didn't let Jewish teachers teach. If he saw a young woman, he'd rip off her marriage wig. If he saw a young man, he'd snip off an earlock. "That's what Mr. Big does, too," he used to say. Then he would beam, get hysterical at his own joke, and shake until the tears came. . . . This made them burn with anger. But nothing could be done. What could Jews do? They did what they always did. They sighed softly, called one meeting after another, trying to think of what to do and how to get rid of such a Haman, the devil take him. They decided to go to my grandfather, Reb Anshel, may he rest in peace. Grandpa Anshel (after whom I'm named) was rich and came from a fine family. He was a follower of a Hasidic *rebbe*, a trustee in the synagogue, a big-shot with the authorities. In brief, a factotum. They came up to him and said: "For goodness sake, Reb Anshel, save the town. Tell us what to do."

My grandfather listened to them and said: "How can I help you, my children? Unless, of course, I can get to see my *rebbe*, may he live and be well. Whatever he'd suggest, we'd do."

No sooner said than done. My grandfather hated long, dragged-out affairs. He wasn't lazy, and money was no object. The town could bear the burden. Where the public's welfare was concerned, how could there be any excuses?

Grandfather Anshel got into his carriage, bade the townspeople goodbye, and left for the *rebbe*'s place one hot summer day. When he arrived, he started telling the *rebbe* the whole story. "It's horrible. It's a catastrophe. We have a man whose hands are clean." The *rebbe* closed one eye and made a motion with his hand, as if to say: hold up. I know everything.

How did he know? Only fools ask such questions. Those *rebbes* knew everything. . . . My grandfather wondered about it, but didn't say a word. He waited for the *rebbe* to speak. A minute later, the *rebbe* called out. "May you be inscribed for a year of health." This astounded my grandfather. How did happy New Year fit in here? Where was the connection? Here it was the height of summer and *Rosh Hashana*, the Jewish New Year, was a long way off. Why the New Year's greeting? But one doesn't question the *rebbe*. Grandfather waited patiently. Before bidding him goodbye, the *rebbe* called him over and said:

"Listen, Anshel" (they were all on a first-name basis with each other, those *Hasidim*), he sighed, "go home in peace and good health. Tell your village that I've wished them a happy New Year. When you arrive home, wait for the big fair. When the fair comes to town, I want you to buy a pair of choice horses, the finest money can buy. I want them to be full-blooded roans. I want both of them to be exactly alike, twins, as if one filly had borne them. They must be completely spotless. Without a freckle. Then, take those horses and hitch them to a carriage, the nicer, the better. Drive them to that city where Mr. Big makes his home. It starts with the letter *P*. When you get there, rest the first day, rest the second day, and rest the third day. The following morning, right after you've said your prayers, and the next afternoon, just before sunset, ride around the palace. But sit in the driver's seat like a lord who's out for a pleasure stroll. And it shall come to pass that, if they stop and ask you: how much do you want for those horses? you will say that you're not a horse-dealer. Now, Anshel," the *rebbe* concluded, "go home, and may God grant you success."

That's exactly what happened. When the big fair came, just like the *rebbe* said it would, my grandfather, Reb Anshel, attended it and bought a pair of full-blooded roans from a gypsy, the likes of which our forefathers never had seen. My grandfather was no connoisseur of horses, but their appearance was made to order—they were exactly alike and spotless, too. Just like the *rebbe* had predicted. After eyeing those horses, my grandfather wouldn't budge. The gypsy, noticing that the horses turned my grandfather's head, naturally put such a price on them that it made Reb Anshel's blood run cold. But there could be no excuses. It was a matter of life or death. The town had to be saved. The Jews had pawned everything they had. He started bargaining with the gypsy—a ruble up, a ruble down. You can be sure that he didn't leave without those horses. He bought them, hitched them to a carriage, and immediately set out for that very place which the *rebbe* had mentioned. He fulfilled everything to the letter. He and the horses arrived in *P* about a month before the start of the Jewish New Year. He rested three days and three nights. Then the next morning after prayers and again before sunset, he drove around the palace gates. He rode slowly. He didn't rush. He had plenty of time and rode back and forth in front of the palace three times. He followed all the *rebbe*'s commands to a *t*.

To make a long story short, he did this one day, two days, three days. Nothing at all happened. He became depressed. What would come of it all? But one mustn't think too deeply about it. If the *rebbe* had said something, surely it wasn't in vain. Listen to what happened! Once, as he was driving in front of the royal palace, he saw a Buttons approaching him, probably one of the adjutants. The adjutant stopped my grandfather, whistling strangely right into his face, inspecting the horses from all angles, like one who understood horseflesh. Then he asked him:

"Listen here, you, how much do you want for these horses?"

Exactly what the *rebbe* said would happen. Reb Anshel's heart leaped a bit, and he answered as he was told to:

"I'm not a horse-dealer."

The Buttons looked angrily at him. "How do you come to such fine horses?"

This time, grandfather was quiet. He didn't know what to say, because the *rebbe* didn't mention a question of that sort. The adjutant became infuriated and said:

"Perhaps you've stolen them, huh?"

Now grandfather's heart sank. I hope everything turns out all right, he thought. But he couldn't say a word. Finally, God inspired him with these words:

"Sir. These horses are mine. I bought them from a gypsy at a fair. I have witnesses. A whole townful of Jews."

"So you have witnesses, huh?" the adjutant said. "I know your sort of witnesses."

Then he started whistling again, looking the horses over. Finally, he said: "You know, the Czar liked your horses."

"What's the drawback?" said grandfather. "If he likes the horses, then my horses can be his horses."

Don't ask how Reb Anshel hit upon an idea like that. If it's fated, God gives you bright ideas. Since he was a wise man, as I've already pointed out, he understood that if the *rebbe* told him to parade around the royal palace, there was a reason for it—as you'll soon see.

Well, in a nutshell, they took the horses' reins, and led those full-blooded roans right into the royal courtyard and showed them to Mr. Big himself. As soon as he saw the horses, he couldn't leave them. Some sort of mystic power was in those animals. He looked at those horses for about an hour, staring at them and showing them off to his entire court. In short, he couldn't get enough of them. He fell in love with them at first sight. Meanwhile, grandfather Anshel was standing quietly on the side, watching the goings-on. He recognized Mr. Big immediately; he knew him from his pictures. But, never mind. It didn't faze him at all. He was just a man, like the rest of them. Then Mr. Big approached grandfather, and as soon as he looked at grandfather, a chill ran through his bones. And when he spoke with his lion's voice, grandfather's heart froze.

"How much do you want for those horses?" Mr. Big asked Anshel.

Grandfather could hardly speak. His mouth was dry, and he felt his voice shaking:

"I don't sell horses. But if his majesty has taken a liking to the horses, and if his majesty will not be angry with me, let the horses be led into his majesty's stables. That's where they belong."

He couldn't say any more, for Mr. Big then looked at grandfather and his soul left him. Then, too, Mr. Big moved closer to Reb Anshel, talking to him. My grandfather practically turned into a heap of bones.

"Listen here. Perhaps you want some special favor. If you do, tell me right now with no bluffs, tricks, flim-flam, or long-winded Jewish commentary. For if you do, it'll cost you dearly."

Well, my dear friends, what do you think went through grandfather Anshel's mind at that time? Surely, the mother's milk in him curdled. But, since Reb Anshel was a brave man, as I told you, it didn't faze him. He plucked up his courage and told Mr. Big:

"Your majesty. King! I swear that I have no underhanded intentions, and I'm not the sort who likes to bluff or trick anyone. I don't ask a thing of his majesty. But I would consider it an honor and the greatest of favors if I could be worthy of having my horses in his majesty's stables and if his majesty would ride them."

Naturally, Mr. Big was moved by these words. He now started talking in a softer tone. His voice, his manner, his words—all changed. He was a new man. Then the Czar left the courtyard and headed for the palace—with grandfather Anshel trailing behind him. It didn't faze him a bit, but his knees shook and his heart ticked like a grandfather clock. Can you imagine—being in the Czar's palace! Wherever you looked, there was only silver and gold and everything was carved out of ivory. Crystal above, marble below, and pure amber on the sides. Amber, the stuff from which pipes and mouthpieces are made. All that wealth made grandfather dizzy, but he controlled himself. Mr. Big walked on with grandfather after him. Then, Mr. Big sat down and asked grandfather to have a seat, too. He offered grandfather a cigar, and grandfather took it and smoked it. It didn't faze him a bit. In the meantime, *she* came in—the Czarina herself, draped in satin and silk and covered from head to toe with diamonds and other valuable stones which sparkled in front of your eyes. She was as beautiful as the Queen of Sheba. So lovely, you couldn't even look at her face. Seeing a Jew in the king's company, comfortable and smoking a cigar, she naturally became very angry and looked sternly at him, as if to say: What's this Jew doing here?

But grandfather Anshel didn't let it bother him. He'd become so high and mighty, nothing bothered him. He continued smoking and didn't so much as glance at her. But she kept staring at grandfather, looking daggers his way. Mr. Big understood that the guest didn't please her, but he ignored it. He looked at her and said cheerfully:

"Dushinka, how about some tea?"

She remained silent.

The Czar repeated: "Dushinka. Tea!"

Again, she remained silent.

The Czar didn't delay, but stamped his foot and roared at the top of his voice: "Dushinka! Tea!"

The window panes shook. It was nothing to sneeze at. Treason, you know. . . . Immediately, adjutants and generals started pouring into the place. In a flash, a boiling samovar, all sorts of home-made jams, egg-bagels, and boiled eggs were ordered. Boiled eggs—for the Czar's court knew that a pious Jew wouldn't touch anything but boiled eggs. The Czar asked him to eat and drink and make himself at home. By and by, he asked grandfather who he was, what he did, how he earned his living, and how the Jews of his area were doing. He wanted to know everything. And he was so friendly, too. Just imagine, grandfather Anshel answered every single question one after the other. When it came to the question about the Jews, he thought: Now's the time to bring up the subject. Now I'll tell him, and I don't care what happens to me. . . . Well, he told Mr. Big everything—and Reb Anshel had just the tongue for it.

"Here's the whole story, your majesty. Your Jews have no complaints. But if his majesty is in a good mood, and if I have found favor in his majesty's eyes, and if his majesty will not be angry at his servant, I shall tell you the whole truth. I'd like you to know, your majesty, that things are all right in your country and that the Jews live by grace of Buttons. If he's just a regular Buttons, it's fine and dandy. But if, God forbid, he isn't, then there's trouble. Not long ago, a new Buttons came into our village—clean as a whistle! And because of that, we're at the end of our rope! There isn't another one like him in the length and breath of your majesty's entire realm. That a Buttons be incorruptible is something unheard of. It's the eleventh plague!"

Mr. Big looked at him and said: "I'll be honest with you. You're talking in riddles and circles and I haven't got the faintest notion of what you're trying to say. What do you mean by—clean as a whistle? And what do you mean by a—Buttons?"

"By clean as a whistle," grandfather said, "I mean a man whose palms won't be greased. By Buttons, I mean a little Mr. Big whom you appoint to watch over every little town. Well, Buttons watches those towns and in a few years becomes very rich. Who from? The Jews, of course. They've gotten used to it. Because just as Jews know they must pray every morning, they also know that an official must take, and a Jew must give. The same idea is found in our holy books. We always kept giving—for sacrifices, for the Temple, here, there. Having been so kind to your servant until now, you will show your grace and hear him out.

"I want you to know, your majesty, that your whole kingdom, from east to west, from north to south, is filled with takers. The only ones whose palms you can't grease are cripples who have no hands. And even he who has no hands, will tell you to slap it down on the table. There's nothing wrong with that, either. You have to live and let live. The Bible tells us to get along with our neighbor. So our commentator Rashi says—but if his dog barks, muzzle him."

Why are you men looking at me? Seems strange, doesn't it, that a Jew should talk this way to a king? Well, take it or leave it. I wasn't there—that any child will understand. But this is the story that my father—may he rest in peace, heard from *his* father. And I assure you that neither my father nor my grandfather Anshel were liars. The long and the short of it was that my grandfather said goodbye to the Czar and went straight to the *rebbe*, reporting back on his trip.

It was just before *Rosh Hashana*. Once in the *rebbe*'s house, he stood (one always stood before the *rebbe*) and told him the whole story from beginning to end. It turned out that grandfather Anshel needn't have bothered, for the *rebbe* knew all about it anyway. Then why did he let him keep talking? Because it wasn't polite to interrupt a man while he spoke. You see, those *Hasidim* are very strict about etiquette. The next day after the Sabbath service, they all sat around the table, waiting for the *rebbe* to speak. But he decided to talk about a verse which had nothing at all to do with the weekly portion of the Torah. Instead, he expounded on a verse from the chapters of admonition against Israel. The people were beside themselves with surprise.

"In the chapter of admonition in Leviticus," the *rebbe* began with closed eyes, as was the custom, "there is a curse, the simple meaning of which we cannot understand. The Bible says that God will send you a nation whose language you will not be able to understand. The question then arises, what sort of a curse is that? Let me repeat it—God will send you someone whose language you won't understand. How is that possible? That the gentiles (forgive the proximity) don't understand our language—well, that's natural—that's why they're gentiles. But that a Jew won't understand what the gentile is talking about? Where's the connection? Is there anything a Jew doesn't understand? If so, we have to interpret the verse differently. God will send forth a nation whose language you will not understand really means that God will send a gentile whom you won't be able to *talk* to. In other words, he'll be as clean as a whistle. His palms won't be greasable. And a gentile who doesn't take bribes is a catastrophe."

That's how the *rebbe* interpreted the verse from the Bible and the crowd was amazed. They licked their fingers and asked for more. Of course, only my grandfather and those close to the *rebbe* understood him. As soon as the Sabbath ended, Reb Anshel set out for home and just made it in time before the start of the Jewish New Year.

Well, listen to this. On the eve of the New Year, when the Jews were leaving the synagogues after prayers and wishing each other a happy holiday, a year of peace and good health—a rumor flashed through town that our Buttons, that our Haman, may he shrivel up, was fired, and in his place the authorities up-on-high had sent a new little Mr. Big, a man clever and wise, good and kind—in short, a jewel of a gentile, a regular Buttons. He took. He was a taker! But he had one flaw (did you ever see anyone completely perfect?) which was discovered later. He had a mighty dry palm. It had to be greased good and heavy. In fact, he took enough for himself and for the Buttons before him. He took from the quick and the dead.

But the upshot was that the Jews had a gay *Rosh Hashana* and an even gayer *Succoth*. Don't even ask about *Simkhas-Torah!* Then the Jews really had a grand time. It was said that even little Mr. Big, that is, the new Buttons himself, had a few drops and danced with the rest of the Jews. Well, it looks like we've arrived at our station. Be well and have a happy . . .

SOMEONE TO ENVY

IN ALL OF Kasrilevke's history, there was no finer funeral than Reb Melekh the Cantor's. Reb Melekh was a pauper, the poorest of the poor, just like the rest of the Kasrilevkite villagers. He received the funeral he did only because he died during the closing service of *Yom Kippur*. Only the saintly die in this manner.

The sun was about to set. It was bidding goodbye to Kasrilevke, shining straight through the old synagogue and lighting up the dead, worn faces, the yellow prayer shawls and the men's white prayer-robes which made them look like living corpses.

These live corpses had long ceased to feel the sensation known as hunger. They just felt their life-strength ebbing. They sat over their prayer book, swaying, refreshing themselves with spirits of ammonia and snuff, singing along with the Cantor.

Reb Melekh the Cantor, a handsome long-bearded, thick-necked man, had been standing on his feet since early that morning. He stood before the Creator with outstretched arms, praying devotedly, crying and pleading for mercy for the people who had chosen him to beg forgiveness for their great sins and ask that they be inscribed for a year of health and peace.

The people in the old synagogue could very well depend on Reb Melekh as intercessor. First of all—his voice. The old townspeople said that in his youth, Reb Melekh had a voice as clear and sharp as the roar of a lion. When he opened his mouth, the walls trembled and the windows shook. As of late, he had become a weeper. He cried as he sang, like a weeping willow, and, looking at him, the whole congregation would burst into tears, too.

As he grew older, his voice became rusty and only the weeping remained—but it was the sort of weeping that could move a wall, or wake the dead.

Reb Melekh lifted his hands, arguing with God in the age-old plaintive melody of the final *Yom Kippur* prayer.

"Oh, Father in Heaven. Oh me! Oh my!"

Hearing this, each person regretted his sins and prayed to God to erase, blot out, forget, and forgive all their transgressions and grant them and their naked, barefoot, and hungry children a good year.

Having reminded themselves of their poor, innocent children, their hearts melted like wax, and they were ready to fast three more days and nights so long as the Eternal One would grant them a year of health.

Meanwhile Reb Melekh rested and caught his breath. Now he cleared his throat and sang a while in his old tremolo, and then resumed his plaintive cry:

"Oh, Father in Heaven. Oh me! Oh my!"

Suddenly, there was silence and the sound of a thump and a fall was heard. Everyone crowded around whispering.

"Come . . . oh . . . sext . . . oh me . . . sexton!"

Khayim the Sexton ran over, then lifted the Cantor. But Reb Melekh's head hung down, his eyes half open, his face white as chalk, his lips ashen. A bitter smile played on his lips.

The whole congregation pressed forward. They put spirits of ammonia under his nose. They sprinkled water on his face. They pressed his temples. But it was no use. Reb Melekh the Cantor was dead.

When a wolf attacks the flock and devours a lamb, the rest of the lambs panic; they go into a momentary panic. Then they press together and begin to tremble all over.

That's what happened in the old synagogue when Reb Melekh died. First a tumult broke out. An eerie scream was heard from the women's section. Tsviya, the Cantor's wife, had fainted. Looking at her, other women fainted, too.

Reb Yozifl, the village rabbi, signaled the trustees and they banged on the prayer stands for silence. Khayim the Sexton (who had led the morning service) went up to the pulpit and continued praying. The whole congregation prayed until Reb Nisel blew the ram's horn which officially brought *Yom Kippur* to a close. They immediately started the weekday evening service. After that, they went out into the courtyard to recite the benediction for the new moon. Then they went home to break the fast. Some did so by eating a quarter of a chicken, a remnant of the previous day's sacrificial fowl. Some did so by having only bread, herring, and water.

An hour after supper, the entire synagogue courtyard was packed with people. There was no room to breathe. Men and women, boys and girls, even babies, had gathered for the funeral.

The villagers themselves took care of the details, not allowing the sextons the privilege. It was no trifle—the Cantor was an important person.

The night was bright and warm. The moon shone down on Kasrilevke, delighted with the poor people who had come to pay their last respects to Reb Melekh the Cantor before he took his long last journey. When the funeral procession stopped in front of the synagogue, Rabbi Yozifl began his funeral oration. And all the people cried.

Rabbi Yozifl quoted the Bible and the Midrash and showed that Reb Melekh the Cantor's death was not that of an ordinary mortal. Only saintly, very saintly, men died that way. Such saints went straight to Paradise. Everyone ought to envy a man as saintly as he, for not all were worthy of dying at the pulpit during the closing *Yom Kippur* prayer, when God has forgiven man's sins. When a man as saintly as he is laid to rest, the entire village must accompany him. When a man as saintly as he dies, the entire village must cry and mourn.

"Cry then, fellow Jews, mourn this saintly man whom we have lost. Beg him to intercede for us before the Seat of Glory. Perhaps he will pray that we all have a year of peace and health. For it is high time that God had mercy on Kasrilevke and its Jews."

Everyone wept. Tears streamed from their eyes and they felt they had sent a fine emissary to God on their behalf.

At that moment, each person wished he were in Reb Melekh's shoes.

It seemed that Rabbi Yozifl forgot that he was addressing a corpse, and finished his funeral oration with these words:

"Well then, go in peace. Stay healthy and lots of luck to you."

For a long time thereafter, the Kasrilevke folk talked about Reb Melekh the Cantor's death and about the fine funeral he had. Mentioning it, they sighed:

"Ah, yes. There was someone to envy!"

AT THE DOCTOR'S

JUST DO ME one favor, doctor. Listen to me until I finish. I don't mean listen to my heart or anything like that. About my sickness, we'll talk later. In fact, I myself will tell you what's wrong with me. I just want you to listen to what *I* have to say, for not every doctor likes to listen to his patients. Not every doctor lets his patients talk. That's a bad habit of theirs—they don't let their patients open their mouths. All they know is how to write prescriptions, look at their watches and take your pulse, your temperature, and your money. But I've been told you're not that sort of doctor. They say you're still young and you're not yet as passionate for the ruble as the rest of them. That's why I came to consult you about my stomach and get your advice. Look at me now and you're looking at a man with a stomach. Medical science says that *everyone* must have a stomach. But when? On condition that the stomach is a stomach. But when your stomach just isn't a stomach, your life's not worth a damn. I know what you'll say next: man must keep living! But I don't need your help for that. *That* got me the taste of the strap when I was a boy in Hebrew school.

My point is that so long as a man lives, he doesn't want to die. To tell you the truth, I'm not afraid of death at all. First of all, I'm over sixty. And second of all, I'm the sort of fellow to whom life and death are the same. That is, sure, living is better than dying, for who wants to die? Especially a Jew? Especially a father of eleven children, may they live and be well, and a wife—despite the fact that she's my third—but a wife for all that. To make a long story short, I come from Kamenitz, that is, not really from Kamenitz proper, but from a little place not far from Kamenitz. I'm a miller—unfortunately—I own a mill. That is, the mill owns me, for you know what they say. Once you're dragged into it, you're finished. You've got no choice. It's a vicious circle and it just keeps on going. Figure it out for yourself. To buy wheat, I have to put up cash. To sell the flour, I have to give credit. I get a note here, a note there and I have to deal with low-down characters and women. Do you

27

like women, doctor? Go give them an account of things! Why this, why that? Why didn't their Sabbath loaf come out well? Well, what fault is it of mine? Not enough heat in your stove, I say. Rotten yeast, perhaps. Wet wood. So what do they do? They step all over you, make mud of you, and swear that the next time their loaves are going to come flying straight at your head. Do you like having breads aimed at your skull? Those are the retail customers for you. But you think the wholesale buyers are any better? Not on your life!

When a wholesale customer first comes into the mill and wants me to give him credit, he flatters and compliments and sweet-talks me to beat the band. He's so butter-soft you can apply him to a third-degree burn. But when it comes to paying, he rattles off a list of complaints. The shipment came late, the flour-sacks were torn, the flour was bitter, moldy, and stale, and a dozen other phony excuses.

But money?

"Money?" he says. "Send me a bill."

In other words, it's as good as half-paid. Send him a bill and he'll say—tomorrow. Send one the next day and he'll say—the day after tomorrow. There's no end to it. The next thing you do is threaten him with a lawsuit and finally you take him to court. You think that settles it? The court gives you a lien on his house. So what? When you get there, the whole place, lock, stock, and barrel is in his wife's name anyway. What can you do? Call him a crook? Well, let me ask you, how can you not have stomach trouble with a business like this? It's not for nothing that my wife says to me: "Give up the mill, Noah, give it up." She's not my first wife, you know, but my third. And a third wife, they say, is like the December sun. But you can't do away with her, she's still your wife, "Give it up," she says, "let it and the wheat business burn to a crisp and then I'll know you're alive and around."

"Ha," I say, "if it only *would* burn. It's insured for plenty."

"I don't mean it that way," she says. "I mean you're always running here and there. For you there's no Sabbath, no holiday, no wife, no children. Why? Why all the tumult?"

For the life of me, doctor, I myself don't know what I'm dashing around for. But what can I do? That's my nature, the deuce take it. I like to panic and rush. What do I get out of it? Headaches, that's all. But I'll take on any business deal you offer. For me there's no bad deal. Bags, wood, auctions. Anything.

You think the mill is my only business? You're mistaken if you do. For you're looking at a man who's a partner in a timber firm, supplies food for the local jail, and has a share in the meat-tax concession—on which I lose money every year. Doctor, I wish you'd make in a month what I lose in a year. Then you'd say I was a friend of yours. So, why bother with it? To spite them all. Me? I'm a man who likes to win out. I don't care if I ruin the whole town and myself included so long as I win out in the end. I'm not such a bad guy at heart, but I have my little whims. I'm a hot-head. When you step on my honor, I'm dangerous. To top it off, I'm a stubborn mule, as well. In the old days, I took my little synagogue to court just for an "Amen" that didn't please me. I was ready to give my all just to see them lose out. And they did. I can't help it. That's the way I am. The doctors tell me it's nerves and it's got to do, they say, with the stomach. Despite the fact that it makes no sense, logically. What connection is there between nerves and the stomach? Strange bedfellows! After all, where are the nerves and where is the stomach? Doesn't medical science say that the nerves are mostly in the brain? And the stomach . . . the devil knows how far away it is! Wait a minute, doc . . . hear me out. . . . I'll be through in a minute. I want to tell you the whole story so that you'll be able to tell me why this plague had to come upon me, my stomach, I mean.

Maybe it's because I'm always scurrying about and am never at home. Even when I am at home, I'm not at home. It's a joke and I'm ashamed to say it—but I swear I don't even know how many children I have and what their names are. A home's no good without a master and without a father. You ought to take a look at my house—knock wood—and see what a mess it's in. It's like a boat without a rudder. The place is in an uproar and a tumult day and night. It's frightening! Eleven kids from three wives, may no harm come to them, is nothing to sneeze at! While one has tea, the other has a snack. When I'm saying my morning prayers, the other one decides to go to sleep. That one filches a potato, the next one wants some herring. This one wants a dairy meal, that one yells his lungs out for meat! After you're washed and sitting at the table ready to say the blessing over the bread—well, there's no knife in sight to cut the bread with. And in the midst of it the little ones are making a racket, fighting with each other, raising all hell—it's enough to make you run away. Why does all this happen? Because I'm never at home and never have any time for them, and my old lady, God bless her, is too good. Well, that is to say, she's not good. She's more of a softie. She can't handle the children. You have to know how to handle them. So they step all over her. She curses, pinches, rips chunks of flesh out of them, but what good is it? She's a mother, after all. A mother's no father, you know. A father grabs hold of a kid and beats hell out of him. That's what my father did to me. Perhaps your father did the same to you, doctor? What do you say? Well, good for you! I don't know . . . maybe you would have been better off without the beatings. What are you squirming about for? I'm going to finish in a moment.

I'm not just barking at the moon, doctor. I want you to know what sort of life I lead. You think I know how much I'm worth? Possibly I'm rich, quite rich. Then again, chances are that—just between you and me—I don't have much at all. I don't know! All day long it's repairs. Like they say: one window pane goes, another comes in its place. You can't help it. Another thing—whether you can afford it or not, you got to give your child a dowry. Especially if God has been kind and you've got grown daughters. All right, doctor, *you* just try and have three grown daughters—God bless them—and marry them off all in one day and then we'll see if you'll be able to sit home and relax for even a day. Now you know the reason for all my running around from pillar to post. And when you rush about like that you catch cold in the train, or gulp down a quick meal in a flea-bitten inn which gives you heartburn and indigestion. And what about all the odors and stale air in the car—isn't that enough to give you a stomach? My only bit of luck is that nature has protected me and I'm not the sickly sort. I've been immune to sickness since I was a boy. Don't mind me being a scarecrow, all skin and bones. That's what my business did for me. Height like mine runs in the family, by the way. We're all tall and thin. I had a few brothers and they were all like me, may they rest in peace. Nevertheless, I was always healthy, never had any stomach trouble, had nothing to do with doctors or illwinds—may it continue that way! But recently they started stuffing medicines and pills and herbs down my throat. Each one comes with a different remedy. This one says: diet, starve yourself. That one says: don't eat at all. You think that's the end of it? Another quack comes along and tells me to eat, but really pack it in. It looks like doctors prescribe what they themselves enjoy doing. I'm surprised they haven't told me to start swallowing rubles yet. They can drive you crazy. One doctor told me to walk a lot. Just get on my feet and head for God-knows-where. Then the other doctor tells me to lie flat on my back and not budge a muscle. Now try and guess which one of them is the bigger ass! You want more proof? One of them kept me on a fifty-two week silver-chloride diet. Pure silver-chloride. When I went to a second doctor, *that* one told me: "Silver-chloride? God forbid! Silver-chloride will be the death of you." So he prescribed a yellow powder, you probably know which one I mean. Then I went to a third doctor and don't you think he took the yellow powder and ripped up the prescription and prescribed an herb? And some herb it was! You can take my word for it that before I got used to that grass I was spitting gall. I used to curse that doctor three times a day, once before each meal when I took the herb. I hope that only half of what I wished him comes true. While taking that herb I used to see the Angel of Death face to face. But what won't a man do for his health's sake? The upshot was that I came back to the first doctor, the one who gave me silver-chloride, and told him the story about the bitter herbs which made my life miserable. He was mad as hell and bawled me out as if I'd stepped on his hat.

"I prescribed silver-chloride," he said. "Silver-chloride! So why are you skipping around like an idiot from one doctor to another?"

"Shh! Tone it down," I said. "You're not alone here. I didn't sign any contracts with you. The next fellow has to make a living too. He's got a wife and family, same as you."

Well, you should have seen him! He blew his stack as if I'd told him God knows what! The long and the short of it was that he asked me to go back to the other doctor.

"I don't need your advice," I told him. "If I want to go, I'll go on my own."

Then I pulled out a ruble and put it on his desk. You think he threw it back at my face? Not at all. They like those little rubles. Boy do they like those rubles! More so than us plain folk. To sit down and examine a patient properly—that they'll never do. They don't let you say an extra word. Recently, I visited a colleague of yours. You know him, so I won't mention his name. I came into his office and before I could say boo he told me to—begging your pardon—strip and lie down on the sofa. Why? He wanted to examine me. Fine and dandy. Examine me! But why can't I say a word? What good does his finger-tapping and pinching do me? But no. He was in a rush. Had no time. He said that there were other people there, on the other side of the door, each waiting for his "next." You doctors have taken up the latest fashions. You have your "nexts" just like the ticket windows at the depot or the stamp lines at the post office. What's that you say? You don't have time either? Oho, now tell me that you *too* have "nexts" waiting out there! You're just a young doctor! Where do you come off having a waiting line? If you continue this way, you hear, you're going to have troubles, not a practice. And you don't have to get hot under the collar about it either. I didn't expect to come here without paying. I'm not the sort of person who'll ask you to do anything for him for nothing. And though you didn't want to hear me out—one thing has nothing to do with the other. I'll pay you for the visit. What's that? You don't want anything for it? Well, I'm not going to force you. You probably have your own source of income. Perhaps you clip bond coupons? Your kitty's swelling, eh? Well, in any case, may God be with you and may the kitty grow and grow. Goodbye! Pardon me if I've taken too much of your time. But that's what a doctor's for.

THREE WIDOWS

1. Widow Number One

YOU'RE SADLY MISTAKEN, my dear sir. Not all old maids are unhappy and not all bachelors are egoists. You think because sitting here in this room, cigar in mouth and book in hand, you know it all; you've probed deep into the soul and you've got all the answers. Especially since, with the good Lord's help, you've hit upon the right word—psychology. Tsk, tsk. You're really something! It's nothing to be sneezed at—psy-cho-lo-gy. You know what the word means? Psychology means parsley. It looks pretty, smells nice, and, if you put in into a stew, it's tasty. But go chew parsley raw! Not interested, huh?

Then why tell me about psychology? If you want to know what psychology *really* is, sit yourself down and pay close attention to what I'm going to tell you. Afterward, you can have *your* say about how unhappiness and egoism began. Here am I, an old bachelor—and an old bachelor I'm going to be until my dying day! Why? There you go! You see, you've asked why and you're willing to listen to me. That shows true psychology! But the main thing is not to interrupt me with questions. As you know, I've always been a bit touchy and lately I've become more nervous. Don't worry—I'm not crazy, God forbid. Madness—that's more up your alley. You're married. I don't dare go *meshugge*. I have to remain sane and healthy. Even you'll admit that. In a word—don't interrupt me with questions. And if something still puzzles you after the telling—complain *then*. All right? Well, here we go. But first let's change seats. If you don't mind, *I'll* sit in the rocking chair. I too like a soft comfortable seat, but you'll be better off in my straight-backed chair. You won't doze off.

Now for the story. I hate long-winded introductions. Her name was Paye, but she was called "the young widow." Why? Here we go with whys! What's so difficult about that? They probably called her "the young widow" because she was young and she was a widow. And think of it! I was younger than her. How much younger? What difference does it make to you? If I say younger, I mean younger. And there were people, with wagging tongues who said that since I was a bachelor and she a young widow . . . you get me? Others even congratulated me and wished me luck. Believe it or not! Even if you don't believe me, it's no skin off my back. I don't have to brag to you! She and I were a couple like you and I are a couple. We just happened to be good friends, no more and no less. We liked each other. Why do I mention it? You see, I knew her husband. Not only did I know him, but we were friendly. That doesn't mean we were friends. I'm just saying we were friendly. Two different things, you know. You can be friendly with someone without being friends. And you can be close friends without being friendly. Anyway, that's my opinion. I'm not asking you what you think.

Well, I was quite friendly with her husband. I played cards with him, sometimes even chess. People say I'm a great chess player. But I'm not bragging. Maybe there are better ones. I'm just telling you what they say. Her husband was a clever, well-versed fellow. He knew his stuff. Self-educated too—no high-school, no college, no diplomas. I'll give you a whole ruble now for all diplomas. What's that you say? No sale? As you wish. I hate to talk anyone into anything.

Her husband was rich to boot, very rich. Although I don't know what you consider rich. In our eyes, a Jew is rich if he has his fully-furnished home, a thriving business, and a carriage to take him to and from town. That's what we call rich. We don't make a big to-do, we don't raise a fuss. We don't aim for the moon. We take it easy. In short, he had a fine business and lived well. It was a pleasure to step into his house. Whenever you dropped in you were welcome. Not like at any other place where they don't know what to do with you the first time you come, the hospitality cools off a bit the second time, and the third time, the reception is so chilly that you catch cold. That's nothing to smile at! I don't mean anyone I know, God forbid. If you come into their house you don't leave without eating and drinking. They treated you like one of their own. You want more? If a button came off your jacket it had to be sewn on on the spot.

You're laughing! You think it's a big joke! A button! What's a button, eh? To a bachelor, my dear friend, a button is an important thing. An entire world. On account of a button a terrible thing once happened. A young man came to look at a girl, a prospective match. The people in the house pointed their fingers at him and laughed. He had a button missing. He went home and hanged himself. But I don't want to get involved in *that* story. I hate to mix one thing with another. . . . Paye and her husband got along so well together. Like a pair of doves. They respected each other much more than some of these highfalutin folk.

But—I don't want to knock anyone. Even if you think I do, what do I care? Here's the story.

One day, Pini, Paye's husband, came home sick and was in bed for five days. On the sixth—no more Pini. Just like that! How? Why? Don't ask! He had a little tumor on his neck. They were supposed to operate on it, but didn't. Why? Y's a crooked letter, that's why. After all, we're blessed with doctors. I brought him two doctors. So they argued with each other. One said operate, the other said don't. Meanwhile, the patient died. Imagine that! You can keep all those doctors. If I made a list of how many people they've sent packing to the next world, your hair would stand on end. In fact, they poisoned my own sister. What do I mean by poisoned? Did they feed her arsenic? I'm not crazy enough to tell you that sort of fairy tale. Poisoned means not giving the proper medicine. If they had given her quinine in time, they might have saved her. Don't start fidgeting now. I haven't gone off the track.

Well, that put an end to Pini. I can't tell you what sort of a blow that was to me. A brother, a father couldn't have mourned him any more. Pini! A part of me died with him. Oh the pity of it, the tragedy. The poor widow's grief! Left with a tiny baby, a little flower, pure gold. Our only consolation! If it weren't for the baby, Rose, I don't see how we could have taken it, she and I. I'm neither a woman, nor a mother who showers praises on babies. But if I tell you that the baby was an exception, take my word for it. Pretty as a picture, she had the best of two beautiful parents. I don't know who was nicer looking, he or she. Pini was handsome, Paye was lovely. The baby had her father's blue eyes. We both loved the baby. I don't know who loved it more, she or I! How is it possible, you ask? She was the mother and I was a stranger. But one thing's got nothing to do with the other. You have to look more deeply into the matter. My connection to the house, my pitying the widow and the innocent little orphans, the baby's charm, and me being as lonely as a stone—take all this, put it together, and you'll have what you call psychology. Not parsley, but pure, unadulterated psychology. Now you'll say I did this because I was in love with the mother. I don't deny that I loved her very much. Do you know how much I loved her? I was always right next to her. I was dying for her. But let her know this?! Not on your life. I spent sleepless nights thinking of how to say it to her. "Listen, Paye, it's like this, you know—I mean, you understand."

But when it came to saying it—I couldn't open my mouth. Go ahead, say that I'm a coward. Say it. What do I care what you say? But think deeply about it—Pini was a true friend of mine. I loved him more than a brother. But here's the problem. Paye! I've just said I was dying for her, haven't I? So the answer is, just *because* I loved her, just because I was crazy for her, just *because* I'd do anything in the world for her—I couldn't say it. But I'm afraid you won't understand me. If I'd have told you *psychology*, you'd have understood. But if I tell you straight from the heart, without any pretensions, then it sounds like a wild tale. But what do I care! You can think what you like. I'm going on my own sweet way and continue the story.

The girl grew up, talked like an adult. A child grows, a tree grows. A radish grows too. But there's a world of difference between one growing thing and another. You have to wait so long to see a baby sit and stand, walk, run and talk! And when it does all these things, are you through? You want me to be an old hen and figure out all the things that can happen to a child: chickenpox, measles, teeth, and so on. But I'm no old hen and won't take up time with any of these silly things. I won't tell you any of her clever sayings. She grew and developed and got smarter each day. I'd say she was like a beautiful rose, if I wanted to express myself like your novelists, who understand a rose like a Turk understands Yiddish. Those novelists are great ones for warming their feet at a fireplace and writing about nature, green forests, the roaring sea, sandy hills, and all sorts of flim-flam about things gone by. I can't stand them and I can't stand their writing. They get on my nerves. I don't even read them. If I get hold of a book and see that the sun shone, the moon floated by, the air was fragrant, the birds tweeted—I fling it across the room. You're laughing, huh? You say I'm a bit touched. All right, then, so I'm not all here. At least it can't get any worse.

Well then, Rose grew up and was, of course, raised properly, as befitted an intelligent family. The mother looked after her education a bit, and I, too, took part. Not a little either, but a lot. Actually, you can well say that I spent all my time with the girl, saw to it that she had the best teachers, that she wasn't late to class, that she took piano lessons and learned to dance. I was everywhere. I, alone. Who else? I handled the widow's affairs too. If not for me, she would have been ruined. As is, our Jews duped her. I know you get mad when I say "our Jews." What else can I say if that's the sort of people they are. You can call me an anti-Semite. It's your choice. It doesn't bother me in the least. I go on my own sweet way. May the anti-Semites have as many plagues as I know what a Jew is. Don't talk to me about Jews. I've had enough dealings with them. You know that I own houses and stores which bring in a large and steady income. I have plenty of contact with them each time it comes to renewing the leases, fixing up the houses, collecting the rent. But the gentiles are no better, though—blast them! However, you would've expected a Jew to be on a higher level. After all—the Chosen People, as we say. You think you're doing them a big favor by singing them this praise. Not at all! What's that you say? You can't stand this? I don't want to start any arguments with you. Whatever you say is fine with me. Every man to his own opinion. I don't care what anyone else thinks. I just know what I think.

Well, where were we? Speaking of the Jews. As soon as Pini died and Paye was left a widow, all sorts of nice people, do-gooders, and advice-givers started streaming to her. They crowded the rooms and wanted to carry away everything she had. But I stood up in time, said, "hold it!" and took all her affairs into my hands. She even wanted me as her partner, but I said: "No! I'm not selling my houses for I don't want any headaches." So she said: "You don't have to sell your houses. You can be a partner just like that." Well what do you think I told her? I told her not to offer me terms like that in the future, for they made me angry. I told her that Pini, may he rest in peace, didn't deserve that I be paid for my help and my time. I didn't want any payment. I had so much time I didn't know what to do with it. When I told the widow this, she remained silent. She lowered her eyes and didn't say boo. If you're subtle, you'll know what I meant by saying what I said. Oh, why didn't I tell her right away? Never ask me why! It just didn't work out. But you can be sure that it would have been as easy as pie. Just one word and we could have been man and wife. But as soon as I started thinking of Pini and what good friends we were . . . I know what you're going to say—that things weren't so red-hot between Paye and me. You're sadly mistaken. I told you before that I was dying for her. And I don't have to start telling you stories about how badly she wanted me, for you're liable to think that . . . but what do I care what you think! You better tell your maid to bring some tea. My throat is as dry as a stick.

Well, then, my dear sir, where did we leave off? The business. Business! That's one thing I'll remember as long as I live. Exploited left and right! Sucked dry! Get that happy look off your face. It wasn't me. It was the widow. No one exploits me. You know why? Because I don't let them. But what difference does it make—letting them yes, or letting them no, if you're with crooks, swindlers, and scoundrels who'll confound anyone. They tried their damnedest to take our money. But know that money isn't taken from me that quickly. They sweated plenty, they spit blood, damn their hides, until they pumped—you want to know how much? As much as they could. Luckily, I noticed it in time and put my foot down. Enough, I said. I started to cut off all transactions, but just while I was cutting them, they cut her head off. And I mean cut. How could I have let them do it, you ask? I'd love to see how a smartie like you would have given those blackguards the slip. Maybe you would've done better. Could be. I won't argue the point. The only thing that can be said of me is that I'm no businessman. I should care! So long as they don't call me a swindler! No doubt you think it didn't cost me anything. But I don't want to brag. I just want

you to know how it all led up to the point where the widow and the
bachelor should have joined forces. Only one word was needed. Just
one. But I didn't say it. Why? Well, listen, that's where the dog lies
buried. Here's where the real psychology begins. The start of a new
chapter called Rose. Listen carefully and don't miss a word, for it isn't
a concocted tale, understand? It's a living, throbbing story, plucked
right out of the heart.

I don't know why, but in each mother there seems to be some sort of
hidden force. It gives her the mad desire to see her daughter engaged
the minute she outgrows her baby clothes. The mother is the picture of
glowing health when she sees young men chasing around her girl.
Every boy is a prospective husband to her. His being a nothing, a faker,
a gambler, and the devil knows what else doesn't bother her at all. You
can be sure that no nobodies and no fakers came within ten feet of us.
Because, first of all, Rose wasn't the type to have anything to do with
those dancers who could do a neat two-step, curl their hands into a
bagel-like flourish, politely scrape their feet, and bow a welcome like
an honest-to-goodness officer. That's one. And, second of all, what
about me? Do you think I'd stand for any run-of-the-mill fly-by-night
getting within looking distance of her? I'd sooner break every bone in
his body. His name would have been mud.

Once I was at a dance with her, at an aristocratic Jewish club. You
know, those you call the bourgeoisie. Well, one of those dudes came up
to her. He bent his elbows like a bagel, tilted his head a bit, and scraped
his little foot. A honey-like smile broke over his face and with a squeaky
girlish voice, he said . . . The deuce knows what he said! He invited her
to dance. You can imagine what sort of a dance he got from me. He'll
remember that dance the rest of his life. Well, we certainly had a good
laugh over that bungler. That taught the fellows a lesson. If they wanted
to meet Rose, they had to meet me first—undergo a little examina-
tion—and then proceed. They nicknamed me Cerberus, the watchdog
who guards the gates of Paradise. Well, it was no money out of my
pocket! But you know who got angry? Rose's mother.

"You're chasing people away from the house," Paye told me.

"What do you mean, people?" I said. "They're not people. They're
dogs."

Well, this happened once, twice, three times, until the roof fell in.
What do you think happened then? Think we had a fight? You're pretty
smart—but you didn't guess this time. Before you start guessing, pay attention.

One day, I came into my widow's place and found a guest there, a
young man about twenty or thirty. There are some sort of young folk—
you can never tell how old they are. This chap, there's no denying it,

was a charming fellow, the sort you take a liking to right away. He had a kind face and gentle eyes. Couldn't complain about him. Do you know why? Because I hate those overly sweet characters with their sugary faces and honeyed smiles. I can't stand looking at those nasty, smiling, yes-men. They'll say yes to an August snowstorm and agree to fish growing on a cherry tree. If I run into someone like that, I just want to smear honey all over him and let the bees have a picnic. You want to know what this young man's name was? What's the difference? Let's say he was called Shapiro. Satisfied? He was a bookkeeper in a distillery, not just bookkeeper, but virtual boss. And, what's more, he had more to say in that place than the real boss. But what's the good of being boss if you don't trust your workers? You may think differently. But I'm not asking you.

In short, they introduced me to this young Shapiro the Bookkeeper, the boss, a sincere boy who played an excellent game of chess. That is, no worse than mine. If you want to think he's a better player than I, go ahead. But I told you I don't make a big chess player of myself. All right, so be a prophet and foresee that there's a whole romance involved. And what a romance! What a passion! What an ass I was not to see it right away. Imagine, I myself added fuel to the fire, praised Shapiro to high heaven, made a fuss over him. May all the chess sets and all the chess-players burn to a crisp! While I kept playing chess with him, his mind was elsewhere. I took his queen and he took my Rose. I checkmated him in ten moves and he checkmated me in three. For his fourth move, that is, the fourth time he came, the widow called me aside. There was a strange light in her eyes as she told me the good news. Things clicked. The match was on. Rose was engaged to Shapiro. My widow was in seventh heaven and gushed with congratulations for me and her and both of us.

I don't want to tell you what happened to me when I heard the glad tidings. You'll say that I'm a gangster, a madman, a lunatic. That's what the widow said, too. First she laughed, then she bawled me out and started crying. This was followed by an attack of hysteria with all the trimmings. What a conflict. Well, the blister finally burst and we had hard words. We didn't spare each other, and in one half-hour we said more truths to each other than we did in our entire twenty-year friendship. I told her quite openly that she was my Angel of Death, that she slaughtered me without a knife, that she'd taken away from me my only consolation, had broken my heart and had taken my soul — Rose — away from me and had given her to another.

She replied that if anyone was an Angel of Death, it was I and no one else, and if anyone had broken another's heart, it was I who broke hers and not all at once either, but slowly, bit by bit, over a period of eighteen years. What she meant by that—well, I don't have to tell you. Any fool would know. I'm not obliged to tell you what I answered. I can only say that I didn't act like a gentleman. That is—I was rude, quite rude. I grabbed my hat, slammed the door, and ran out like a madman. I gave my word that I'd never set foot in that house again. Well, what do you think? You're a scholar of sorts. What does your psychology have to say for that? What was I to do next? Drown myself? Buy a pistol? Or hang myself on a tree? It's obvious that I neither drowned, shot, nor hanged myself, thank God. As to what happened later, we can save that for another time. You won't burst if you wait a while. I have to be off to my widows. They're expecting me for supper.

2. Widow Number Two

Why'd I let you wait so long? Because I wanted to. When I tell a story, I tell it when I want to *tell* it, not when *you* want to *hear* it. It's obvious that you want to hear it pretty badly. Everyone wants to listen to a story, especially a good one. After all, what do you care if you sit at home smoking an after-dinner cigar in a comfortable chair while I tear my lungs out talking. The fact that the teller eats his heart out—what's that to you? So long as you hear a fine tale. No, no, I don't mean you, don't get scared. You just pay close attention to what I'm telling you. Despite the fact that what I shall tell you now has nothing to do with what I told you last time, I'd still like you to remember what I said, because there is a little bit of a connection between them. Not only a little, but a lot. If you've forgotten anything, I'll remind you. In fact, I'll tell you the whole story in a nutshell.

I had a friend Pini, who had a wife Paye, who had a daughter Rose. Pini died, leaving Paye a widow. I was a friend of the family, a secretary, a brother. I was mad about her. But I didn't have the courage to tell her. So passed the best years of our lives. Her daughter grew up, the rose bloomed, and I was a lost soul. Completely lost. Then out of the blue there came Shapiro the Bookkeeper who didn't play a bad game of chess and Rose fell for him. So, I poured all the stored-up bitterness within me onto the mother, had a fight, slammed the door, and swore never to set foot in their house again. Happy now?

Now I know that you want to know one thing. Did I keep my word? But after all, you're a . . . what do you call it . . . a psychologist. In that case, *you* tell *me*—was I supposed to keep my word or not? Aha! You're not saying a thing. Do you know why? Because you don't know. Here's what happened.

I roamed all over town that night, like a maniac. I measured the length and breadth of each street at least three times, came home at dawn, looked over all my papers, tore many of them up—I hate old papers, you see—packed my things and wrote letters to a few acquaintances. I have neither friends nor relatives, thank goodness. I'm as lonely as a stone. I left instructions about the disposal of my houses and stores, and when I finished doing all this, I sat down on my bed, held my head, and thought and thought and thought until sunrise. I washed, dressed, and went to see my widow. I rang the bell, was admitted, told the maid I'd have some coffee until Paye got up. My widow got up and when she saw me, she stood without moving, her face pale, her eyes puffy. It seems that she too didn't get too much sleep that night. The first thing I said were these three words. "What's Rose doing?"

As I said this, Rose herself came in, lovely as the day, bright as sunshine, good as God. Seeing me, she blushed, then came up to me and patted me on the head, just like a baby. Then she looked into my eyes and burst out laughing. What do I mean by that? It was not an insulting laugh, but one which so charmed you that soon you, the world, the very walls were laughing. Yes, my dear friend, that's the sort of power she has to this day. For her laughter I'd give away everything I have. Even now! The only trouble is, she doesn't laugh any more. She has her troubles, poor thing, and ah me, there's no room for laughter. But I hate to put one thing before another. I like things to be in their proper order. In that case, let's proceed in order.

Do you know what it's like to marry off a daughter? You don't? Then you're better off! I know very well what it's like, even though it was someone else's daughter. I'll never forget it. What was I supposed to do, I ask you, if my widow Paye was the sort of woman who was used to having everything prepared for her? Whose fault is it if not mine? I taught them, mother and daughter both, that if they ever needed anything, all they had to do was tell me and, although the world turned upside down, they'd have it within the hour. Money—they came to me. Need a doctor—they came to me. Hire a cook—me. A dancing instructor—yours truly. Clothes, shoes, a tailor, butcher, baker, candlestick maker—me. A pen, a pin, a screw, me, me, me. Don't you think I told them, "what's going to become of you? A dish rag!" That's what I told them, but they laughed. Everything was one big joke. There are people like that, you know. Not many, but they're around. It's my luck that their path had to cross mine. Who had to play nursemaid to others' children? Me! Who had to go *meshugge* with other peoples' troubles? Me! Who had to dance at others' weddings? Me! Who had to mourn at others' graves? Me! Who asked you to, you say. But my answer is, who asks you to run into a burning house and save someone else's child? Who asks you to jump into the water when another is drowning? Who asks you to make faces when someone else is in pain? You'll probably say that you don't run, jump, or make faces. Well then, you're an animal. I'm no animal. I'm human. I don't make myself out to be an idealist. I'm an ordinary, run-of-the-mill person and a confirmed old bachelor to boot. Despite the fact that your psychology says that an old bachelor is an egoist. Maybe that in itself is egoism. What's that? You hate that sort of philosophizing? Me, too. All right, then, we had to marry off my widow's daughter, Rose, and I had to make believe I was one of the family. Did I have a choice? And knowing me and my quirks you know how much I liked that. I hate that expression, "one of the family." Call me lackey, servant, footman, call me whatever you like, but don't call me "one of the family." But my widow was all aglow with the new name she had — "in-law." Call her "in-law" and she melted with joy. "Well, you'll soon be a mother-in-law," I told her. She lit up like a bulb. "I hope I live to see it," she said. What a mother-in-law! You should have seen her at the wedding. Pretty as a picture. And young, too. You'd never guess they were mother and daughter. You'd swear they were sisters. I just kept staring at her under the bridal canopy and thought: What an idiot you are! You lonely old character. Here's your chance. With just one word you can stop being lonely. With just one glance . . . you'll build your own home, plant your own garden . . . and you'll step into Paradise. You'll live a peaceful life among your own true loved ones. Get Rose out of your mind. Rose isn't for you. Rose is a baby compared to you. Don't be foolish. Look at the mother! Just say the word, you dumb ass. Tell *her* and no one else. What are you dilly-dallying for? Can't you see how she's looking at you? Just look at her eyes!

That's what I said to myself as I met Paye's eyes and I felt part of my heart breaking. I felt such pity for her. You listening? Pity was what I felt. Nothing more than pity. There was a time I had another feeling. Now, only pity remained. But talking of pity, maybe I'm to be pitied too. And maybe I more than her? Did I owe her something? Why did she keep still until now. Why was she silent now? Where is it written that I had to tell her and that she couldn't tell me. Shyness, you're going to say. The way of the world. That's the way convention has it. Well, I laugh at your convention. It makes no difference to me if *he* or *she* says it first. People are people. If she says nothing, I say nothing. You want to call it stubbornness, ambition, lunacy? Call it what you will. I told you once before that it makes no difference to me. I'm pouring my heart out to you because I want us both to analyze it and find out where the loose screw is. Maybe the answer is that Paye and I had never been alone for two minutes. There was always someone else around who took up our time, our thoughts, our feelings, our troubles, and our joys. All these belonged to others, not to us. But that we be alone together — not on your life! It's as if we were both made to cater to others. First it

was Pini. Then the good Lord sent us little Rose. Now he'd sent us another bundle of joy: a freeloading son-in-law. But he was the right man.
Any Jew would want a son-in-law like him. You know, I'm not easily
impressed and don't flatter the next fellow. I don't overdo songs of
praise or exaggerate compliments. I'll just say that the word "angel" was
an insult to the young man. Satisfied? If there is a heaven and if angels
do flutter around up there, and if those angels are no worse than
Shapiro, then I tell you it pays to drop dead and be with them rather
than with the two-legged beasts who spend their time down here under
God's skies and pollute the earth. I'll bet you'll say that I'm a misanthrope, a hater of mankind. If people would treat *you* the way they've
treated *us*, you wouldn't be a misanthrope but an out-and-out cut-
throat. You'd take a knife, stand smack in the middle of the street, and
kill people like sheep. And, anyway, what sort of queer tradition do you
have here, letting a man talk for hours on end and not even offering
him a glass of water. Tell the maid to make tea.

Well then, where was I? Our bundle of joy, Shapiro. I've already told
you he was the manager of a distillery. Not only manager, but over-all
boss. Everything was under his supervision, everything was in his
name. You can't imagine how much they trusted him. They loved him
like a son. It's not hard to imagine that the two owners, partners and
crooks (they'll forgive me since they're long time residents of the other
world—America) were big shots at the wedding. They gave him a
chestful of silver, made themselves out to be open-hearted and kind,
like honest-to-goodness philanthropists. And you know how much I
adore philanthropists, especially if they're bosses who come to my party
and display their philanthropy for all to see and show everyone that they
appreciate another man's work. Perhaps because of him they had become rich? If it weren't for Shapiro, those two probably wouldn't be
philanthropists today. Wipe that smile off your face. It's uncalled for.
My dear sir, I don't make myself out to be a socialist, but I hate a philanthropic boss. Why do I say this? Do I have any proof? You'll soon
hear what a philanthropic boss can do. You'd think if with God's help
you had a good business, which brought in several thousand rubles
each year, and if you had a man you could trust as your first-hand assistant, you wouldn't lose any sleep at night. You could even go abroad
and have a wonderful time. But you know "our Jews." Yes, I know, you
hate that term, but I'll say it again. "Our Jews." They never have
enough. A Jew likes to do business, run around, finagle, brag, put on a
big show. Let everyone see! Let everyone hear! In short, my Shapiro's
bosses weren't satisfied with having such a top-notch business in such
sure hands. They started investing in forests and lots; they went into
auctions and mortgages, into wheat and corn. They got a mad desire to

creep into real estate. There was a rush for real estate. They burned
with excitement until they themselves were burned up and dragged our
Shapiro into the mess with promissory notes. They grabbed whatever
cash there was and ran off to America. Folks say they're doing all right
for themselves over there. But they left Shapiro with debts up to the
neck, notes which he himself had signed. Every single one. There was
a big scandal, and it reached the point where they didn't care whether
he was just an employee or boss—he had to cover the notes. But since
he didn't have a kopek, he was bankrupt. And since he couldn't show
that he was bankrupt due to some extraordinary misfortune, it was
called fraudulent bankruptcy. In other words, he was a rogue and
rogues were clapped into jail because the world hates a rogue. You can
go bankrupt a dozen and one times so long as you do it correctly and
with finesse. Why, then you can thumb your nose at the public. You
buy yourself a house with all the trimmings, become one of the town's
elite. You arrange the finest marriages, you air opinions left and right,
you step on other people's toes, you elbow your way into high society,
all the way into the four hundred who lead the town by its nose. You
think you're great, you huff and puff with pride, you swell like a turkey,
you don't recognize old friends, and you become so impressed with
yourself that the deuce himself almost takes you. You'll pardon me, but
you understand that it's not you I mean. I'm just talking to the wall.
The long and short of it was that my boy Shapiro couldn't take this hu-
miliation—and another thing—he was all upset about the poor widows
and orphans (His bosses, you see, didn't spare anyone. They grabbed
whatever they could.) He took poison.

I don't think what he took and where he took it from should make
any difference to you. And why poison in the first place? And what sort
of letter did he write me? What did he say? And how did he bid goodbye to Rose and me and the mother? All these things are just senti-
mental eyewash which the novelists use to squeeze tears out of silly
readers. In a word: he not only poisoned himself, he poisoned all of us.
We three were so broken up, so deep in grief, so numb with pain that
we didn't even shed a tear. Not a one of us. We were stunned, dumb-
founded. We were as good as dead. We would have been the happiest
people alive if someone had come and chopped all our heads off with
one blow. You listening? You can say what you want—I can't stand
those who come to console you after a tragedy. Their make-believe sad
expressions which say: Thank God it isn't me. Their wooden talk
which makes no sense, their false praises, their long faces when they
leave. You want more? You know, it's customary for every young lout on
such occasions to look into the Book of Job, although they can't make
head or tail out of it. Even that custom sickens me. What's that? I'm a

heretic? Is that heresy in your eyes? And what about tripping up an innocent fellow, getting him to sign promissory notes and then sneaking off to America and leaving the other fellow to poison himself and three other innocent folk—what would you call that? Isn't that heresy? And wouldn't you label that an unjust act of God? But how can you complain against God? Well look and see what this very same Job has to say, that book which everyone reads, but no one understands. You're not saying a word, eh? Me, too, for you can talk until you burst and no one'll give you the answer. You can rehash the words: The Lord gave and the Lord has taken away—until you're blue in the face, and you won't be any the wiser. What's that you say? Philosophizing is like chewing straw? My very words!

Now, back to the widow. What am I saying, widow? I mean my two widows. Rose, a widow too! That's a laugh. It was fate's cruel joke. It was so tragic that one could only laugh. Rose a widow! You should have seen her. A fifteen-year-old couldn't have looked younger. A widow! But that's not all. Rose was a mother, too. Three months after Shapiro's death the baby came and the house was full of its sounds. They called her Feygele and she became queen of the household. Everything was done for Feygele. Wherever you walked or sat or went it was only Feygele, Feygele, Feygele. If I were religious and believed in Providence, as you call it, I'd say that God rewarded us for our suffering and sent the baby as consolation. But you know I'm not much of a believer, and I have my doubts about you, too. What's that? You want to convince me that you *are* a believer? Fine and dandy. I don't care. So long as you yourself are sure that you're no hypocrite. Listen! I hate Jewish hypocrites as much as a good Jew hates pork. Be as religious as ten thousand demons, but be sincere about it. If you're a faker, a saint in masquerade, then you're not one of my boys and you can fry in hell for all I care and I have no further use for you. That's the sort of guy I am!

Where were we? Oh yes, Feygele. As soon as Feygele appeared, everything blossomed, everyone smiled and was happy. All our faces shone. Our eyes brightened. One with the baby, we were all born anew. And what's more, Rose, who hadn't smiled for ages, suddenly began to laugh her strange old laugh which charmed you into laughter too—although you really wanted to cry. That's what Feygele did when she opened her eyes and looked at us with the first gleam of understanding. Not to mention the first time we saw a smile on her lips. Both widows practically went out of their minds with astonishment. When I came, they ran to me with such vigor that I was scared half to death.

"Oh, where were you a minute ago?" they pounced on me.

"What is it? What happened?" I asked, frightened.

"Why just half a minute ago Feygele laughed. Her first laugh."

"Is that all?" I said coldly. But deep down I was very happy, not so much for the smile but because my two widows were so overjoyed. Well now you can imagine what happened when she started teething. The young widow, Rose, was the first to feel it. So she called the older widow, Paye, and they both tested it with a glass to see if it was really a tooth. When they were sure it was, they made such a tumult that I ran in from the next room with my heart in my mouth.

"What happened?"

"A tooth."

"It's your imagination," I said purposely, to tease them. Then both widows took my finger and made me feel the little point in Feygele's warm mouth which could be—which *was*—a tooth.

"Well?" they both asked and waited for me to bring regards from the tooth. I played innocent. I loved teasing them. I asked:

"Well what?"

"Is it or isn't it a tooth?"

"Of course. What did you expect?"

Since it *was* a tooth, why then Feygele was a genius the likes of which hadn't been seen on earth. And being a genius, she deserved to be kissed until she started to cry. Then I tore the baby out of their arms and quieted her down, for I soothed her best of all. In fact, you can well say that she liked my hair better than anyone else's. Her tiny fingers liked to mangle my nose better than any other nose in the world. Feeling those little fingers was seventh heaven. You longed to kiss each part of those white and tiny, smooth and soft little fingers a thousand times. I know you're looking at me and thinking: he's a woman at heart. For if he weren't he wouldn't love children so much. A good guess, right? Here's the story. What I am at heart, I don't know. But I do know that I love children. That's a fact. Who, then, are you supposed to love if not babies. You want me to love those adults with the double chins and packed pot-bellies whose whole life is one long lunch, Havana cigar, and game of cards? Or do you want me to love those noble-hearted public servants who live off the community's kitty while they raise a racket and holler to beat the band that all their labors are for the public good? Or perhaps you want me to love those sweet young things who want to change the world, who call me a "bourgeois" and want to make me sell my houses and divide it with them in the name of expropriation? Or perhaps you'll tell me to love those bloated women, those fattened cows whose only ideals besides clothes, diamonds, and the theater are eating and flirting with other men? Perhaps you want me to adore those short-haired old maids who were called "nihilists" in my day and today operate under other dandy nicknames? Go ahead, say it:

I'm such a grouch and such a misanthrope because I'm an old bachelor. And that's why I don't like anyone. Say what you want. It doesn't bother me in the least. I'll just keep on talking.

Where was I? Oh yes, Feygele and how we loved her. All three of us devoted ourselves body and soul to that baby, for it sweetened the bitterness in our lives. It gave us fresh energy to carry the yoke of this foolish and botched-up world. For me, especially, the child was a source of secret hopes. You'll understand what I mean if you remember what Rose meant to me. The more the baby grew, the more the hope grew in my heart that my loneliness would once and for all be ended and I too would know what a normal life was. I wasn't alone with that thought. This same hope budded in Paye's heart, although we never mentioned it. But it was as clear as day to all three of us that someday it would have to be. You'll ask: how can people understand one another without talking? Well that shows that you really know psychology. But not people! I'll paint you a picture and you'll see how people can talk without words and read each other's eyes.

It's a summer night. The milky-way streaks the sky. I wanted to say that the stars glittered, sparkled, shone. But, then I remembered that that's the way it's written in a book. I don't want to rehash anyone else's words. I've told you already that I hate their descriptions of nature. They resemble nature as much as I do the Turkish Sultan. Anyway, it was a summer night, one of those rare and warm, clear and beautiful nights which makes a poet out of the least sensitive soul and makes him long for something he cannot put his finger on. Some sort of holy spirit fills him and he sinks into a sacred calm. He stares into the deep blue skullcap which we call the sky and feels that it is whispering secrets to the earth, continuing that eternal dialogue which people call godliness.

Well, what do you say to my descriptions of nature? You don't like them? Well, now I'm exposed! But wait, you're not through yet! I forgot to tell you about the beetles—queer, fat, brown beetles which come in the dark, beating their wings, humming and buzzing and bumping into the walls and windows, then falling to the floor, their skirts damaged. There, they finally quiet down. But don't worry . . . they'll rest for a while on the ground then start the whole business all over again. Now, all four of us were sitting on the porch, facing the garden. Feygele was big, she would soon be four, and she was talking like a grown-up. She talked and asked questions. Loads of them. Why is the sky the sky, the earth the earth? When is night and when is day? Why is it dark at night and light during the day? Why does Mama call Grandma "Mama" and why does Grandma call Mama "Rose"? Why am I her uncle and not her father? Why does Uncle look at Grandma and Grandma at Mama and why is Mama red in the face? You can imagine what laughs this caused.

When Feygele asked what we were laughing about, we laughed even more. The result is, we looked at each other and knew quite well the meaning of that look. We needed no words. Words were unnecessary. Words were made only for babblers, women, and lawyers. Like Bismarck once said: "Words were given to us to hide our thoughts." Animals, birds, and other creatures, don't they get along without speech? The tree grows, the flower blossoms, a blade of grass sprouts, stays close to the earth, kisses the sunbeam—where's their speech? Eyes, my dear sir, human eyes are great things. What eyes can tell you in a minute, a mouth will never say in a day. Our looking at one another that night was a page, a chapter in our mutual history. Better yet, it was a poem, a song, the pathetic song of three lost lives, three crippled souls, who because of various entanglements couldn't drink from the fountain called happiness and from the spring called love. . . . Unwittingly, I've just come out with the word love. Believe me, it disgusts me. You know why? Because your writers use this sacred word so often it becomes a workaday expression. When your writers use the word "love," it's sacrilege. The word "love" has to pour out of you like a prayer to God. It has to flow forth in a song without words, in a song of pure poetry. And it doesn't have to rhyme either. When I read rhymes like moon-June, love-dove, and other such stuff your poets dream up, it seems that I'm gulping raw beans followed by a dessert of blotters. You may not like my image, but you don't have to make a face. In a minute I'm going to finish the story of widow number two and I'm going to make it quick, for I hate people yawning in my face.

Tell me, did you ever have a toothache so bad that the tooth had to come out? But instead of pulling it right away, you put it off from day to day until, with heavy heart, you finally go to the dentist. You come to his office and see the sign on his door: Doctor So-and-so—office hours from 8 to 1 and 1 to 8. You look at your watch and say to yourself: then what's my rush?

You turn around and head for home, but, meanwhile, your tooth is killing you. Well, that's exactly how it was with me and Rose. I left my house every morning with the thought that it had to happen today and no excuses. First I'd talk it over with my widow number one. She'd blush, lower her eyes, and say, "It's all right with me. Now talk it over with Rose." Then I'd leave widow number one and go to widow number two and say: "Listen, Rose, here's the story." Well, with that in mind, I grabbed my hat and came to my widow's house. Feygele came running into my arms, threw her hands round my neck, kissed my glasses, and begged me to ask Grandma and Mama—they'd listen to me—that she not go to school or play or dance that day, but be allowed to go to the zoo with Uncle. They had brought new monkeys, monkeys so funny your sides hurt from laughing. Well, how could you refuse and not take her to the zoo to see the funny monkeys?

"What's going to become of the child?" widow number one grumbled.

"He's spoiling the child," widow number two echoed.

And Uncle paid no more attention to the two widows than to the man in the moon. He took Feygele and went to the zoo and introduced her to the new monkeys whose antics made you roll with laughter. That's the way it was. There was a different alibi every time. Days passed. Weeks. Years. The child got older, began to understand things you don't speak of. It was a sort of silent agreement among us three that we'd wait until the girl grew up. When Feygele would grow up and pick her mate, our hands would no longer be tied. Then we'd set our lives aright and build a new home for ourselves. Everyone made plans— each in his own heart—about how we would live together. The young couple—Feygele and her husband. The old couple—Rose and I. And the widow—Grandma Paye—would rule over us all. What a life that would be! The only problem was—when would we see it come true? We couldn't wait for Feygele to grow up, pick a young man, and marry. Like the saying has it: keep living and you'll live to see it. I hate clichés like that. Do you like them? Wonderful! Enjoy yourself!

Well then, keep living and you'll live to see it. Feygele grew up, matured, chose a husband. And *there's* where the dog lies buried. Here's where your real psychology begins. You know, looking at your watch is entirely uncalled for. I won't tell you any more today in any case. I have to go now. My widows won't know what to think. If you want to hear the story of widow number three, I don't mind if you pick yourself up and come to visit me. If not—it's up to you. I won't drag you over by the coat-tails. You'll come of your own free will. So long!

3. Widow Number Three

It's good you came at a time when I'm at home. What I mean is, I'm always at home. For myself, not the next fellow. Every man has his own habits. For instance, I'm used to having the cat sit opposite me when I eat. I won't eat without my cat. Here she is. Kootchie-kootchie-koo! What do you say to her? Smart as a whip. She'll never help herself to anything. Even gold. Do you like her fur? What's that? You hate cats? Silly old prejudice, a remnant of Hebrew-school days. Don't tell me! Don't make excuses. How do you like your tea? With milk or plain? I take it with milk, too. Scat . . . beat it, puss. The deuce take it!! There's nothing she likes better than milk. She won't go near butter, but once she spots milk, she must take a lick.

You know I hate long-winded introductions, but here I have to say something. I hate when people smile. Laugh as much as you please. But don't smile. Do you remember everything I've told you? If you don't, don't be bashful. People smarter than us also forget sometimes. It looks like I'll have to give you a quick résumé of what happened. I had a friend, Pini, who had a wife, Paye, who had a baby girl named Rose. Then Pini died, and Paye was left a widow. I became one of the family. We both loved each other. But we never spoke of it. Kept it to ourselves. So passed our best years. Meanwhile, her daughter, Rose, grew up and I was mad about her. Then in slipped a Shapiro, a good bookkeeper and a fine chess player. Rose fell for him. I had a fight with Paye and left thinking I'd never again set foot in that house. I didn't keep my word and came back on the next day and once again made myself at home. I masqueraded as "one of the family" and we celebrated the wedding of Rose to Shapiro, the boy who managed his bosses' business, even signed their notes. They pulled a fast one and ran off to America, leaving him with their debts. He committed suicide and Rose remained a widow.

Now there's two widows. Just as Paye, my widow number one, was left with a baby after Pini's death, so Rose was left with a baby after Shapiro's death. We loved the baby and were so devoted to her that we didn't have time to think of my romance with widow number two, Rose. We put it off until Feygele grew up. Well, when she finally got older . . . Look, do me a favor! When I'm telling a story, don't read! It's a disgusting habit! You better listen to what I'm saying, for there's a new story beginning.

You can say what you like about me, but I've never been fanatic or stubborn. I've always kept up with the times. I never went backward nor stood still like others, who always complain about the modern generation and their newfangled ideas.

I can't stand these old wiseguys with their eternal pretensions who say: look at the egg starting to teach the hen. Who came first, the chicken or the egg? What a bunch of asses they are! On the contrary. Just *because* it's younger, is the egg better, smarter, more skillful. The older generation must listen carefully to the younger, because they're fresh out of the shell. They study, they desire, they seek, they find, they accomplish. What else? Want them to be like you, moldy old scholars who sit themselves down on books from the year one and refuse to budge? The only think I'm angry at the young ones about is that they belittle us, they push us completely out of the picture. They don't even call us asses and donkeys. We're nobodies. We don't exist. We're not even here. And that's the end of that. Just imagine, three young popinjays come into our place. I mean the widows' place. And they didn't come to see the widows either, but the granddaughter, Feygele. Whether they're students or not, the devil himself knows. But they wear black shirts, they don't have haircuts, they don't introduce themselves, they have sharp tongues and Karl Marx is their god. He's not their Moses mind you, but their god. Well, what do I care? Let him be their god. I'm not going to do myself in on account of that. Especially since I myself am close to the socialist ideal. I'm also familiar with capital, the proletariat, economic struggle, and all that. And if you want to know—I myself—get that smile off your face. No, I don't belong to any organization, God forbid. But I'm certainly not a down-at-the-heels tailor, either.

Well then, these three characters came to visit us every day. One's name was Finkel, the second was called Bomstein, and the third, Gruzevitsh. They came and felt perfectly at home. That's the way my two widows are. When a visitor came they didn't know what to do first. They went all out for them, especially bargains like those three, one of whom was surely a candidate for Feygele. What I mean is, they were all candidates, but she couldn't marry three of them, so one of them it had to be . . . But go guess which one it was if the thing was never even mentioned. Nothing was sure. They asked no one. Who were they to ask? The mother? What did they give a hang about the mother? She was a young woman with a pretty face and that was the end of that. The grandmother? Who was she? She was only a hostess who had to see to it that there was enough to eat and drink when they came visiting. Not only eat and drink, but glut and guzzle. Me? I don't come into the picture at all. What am I to them? An extra seat at the table. No more than that? You'd think they'd throw a word my way? Unless of course it was: pass the salt, pass the sugar, or, got a match? And all that without a please or a thank you. If they wanted a match they'd make a striking motion with their hands, or they'd stick out their lips while I was smoking a cigar—just like speaking to a deaf-mute. Aside from that—not a word. Sometimes they came and found only me in the house. So they sat down in a corner and talked to each other, or sprawled on the sofa and yawned. You'd think they'd say something just to be polite. But no. Just as if I wasn't there. Certainly, I wouldn't start talking to them first. I'm not like the others who slipped them ten thousand little flatteries, a load of sweet talk and sugar-coated smiles. The guy I'm going to kowtow to hasn't been born yet. And it's not because I'm such a proud one either. All right, let's say I am proud. Call it what you want. You can keep your opinions to yourself. But bragging is one thing I hate. I just want to tell you the sort of breed those three big-shots were. Once, when I came out and asked if any of them played chess, you should have seen the looks on their faces. You should have heard them cackling. I thought, what sort of crime is it to be a socialist *and* a chess player, too. Karl Marx won't turn over in his grave. But there's no talking to them. I don't give a damn about them. They can go straight to hell for all I care. But I was burned up at Feygele—why did she laugh along with them? Why should every single thing they said be sacred to her, as if they were God's own words at Sinai? What sort of pagan worship was it these young folks practiced? What sort of new fanaticism? A brand new *Hasidic* movement! Karl Marx was the *rebbe* and they were his devotees. And after Marx was there no one? Where were Kant, Spinoza, Schopenhauer? Where were Shakespeare, Heine, Goethe, Schiller, Spenser, and hundreds of other great men who also had something clever to say? Of course they weren't as wise as Karl Marx, but at least they didn't prattle nonsense. I must tell you that I'm not one to let a fellow spit into my face. I hate stuck up folk and I love making them angry. If they say black, I'll say white. On purpose. And go fight me if you want. Once I heard them say that Tolstoi was a nobody. I'm not a Tolstoi fan. Not one to make a god of him and his new philosophy which makes of Jesus something he never was. But as an artist, I think Tolstoi is on the same plane as Shakespeare. If you don't agree with me, I'm not going to eat my heart out. You know me. So, I purposely brought Feygele one of Tolstoi's books to read. You ought to see the face she made as she pushed Tolstoi aside. What's the matter? Finkel, Bomstein, and Gruzevitsh—none of them liked Tolstoi.

Then I really blew my top. When I have to, you see, I can be a meanie. I made mud of all three of them. I told them that Karl Marx was a theory and that theories change. Today it was this theory, tomorrow that one. But Tolstoi was a great artist and art remains forever.

Well, you should have seen them flare up. If you had provoked the Baal Shem Tov himself, his disciples couldn't have been angrier. The long and short of it was, if my two widows hadn't interfered there would have been a royal scandal. But, I saw later that I was an ass. After all, I should have apologized to them! You know why? Because Feygele wanted it that way. And if that's what she wants, that's what it'll have to be. If she tells me today to pick up the house and move it, don't you think I'd do it?

That girl not only charmed me, but made me a devoted slave. She destroyed my will and made a robot of me. Mine wasn't the only head she turned. She put us all into a dither with the match she made. She picked Gruzevitsh, a chemical student in his third year. He wasn't a bad chap, but nothing extraordinary. There were plenty worse. But first of all, he came from a fine family. That's very important. Say what you will, but it counts in the end. Don't get excited—I didn't mention noble lineage! I can only say that who you stem from counts. If you come from a bunch of louts, I don't care how educated you are, you'll still remain a lout. I'm not going to talk about his other qualities. Their sort—to give the devil his due—are good and honest and noble so long as they keep true to themselves. But as soon as they step out into the big wide world and become somebodies, watch out! They're worse than anyone else. If a nobody puts one over on you, he'll hide. If a somebody swindles you, he'll show you logically that you're the swindler, not he. But why lose time with silly philosophizing! At the age of seventeen, our Feygele became Mrs. Gruzevitsh. I won't chew your ears off with long stories about the wedding, who arranged it, who paid for it, and the tumult in the widows' place. The mother lived to bring her consolation to the wedding canopy. The grandmother had the joy of seeing her grandchild married. And me? The fool! What sort of joyous occasion was it for me? That the youngest one had been married off? But listen to this. Our entire joy lasted no longer than *Purim*. The third day after the wedding, Gruzevitsh was taken to jail over a small matter. They just happened to run across a whole storehouse of bombs and dynamite. And since he was a chemist, and a famous one at that, suspicion fell on him. In addition, a few of his own letters had been found. In short, they took him in.

I had my work cut out for me. I ran from pillar to post, greasing palms, and got headaches and plagues. It didn't do a bit of good. Once caught in a mess like that, you might as well kiss everyone goodbye. Picture the suffering of the little seventeen-year-old girl. The anguish of her mother, Rose, and of the grandmother. The wrath of God fell on that house.

And let me tell you, business was none too good, either. I started feeling the pinch in my pocket. I became frisky, schemed and swindled, mortgaged some of my houses, and the money just melted away. When the cash went, I sold a few of my stores outright. I'm not telling you how clever I was and I'm not bragging. I just want to show you what my widows were like. They gave no thought to what they were living on, where the money was coming from, and what they'd do for future support. It didn't concern them in the least. I had to worry about everything. Everything had to be on my shoulders. I had to knock myself out. Who asked me to? God knows! It came by itself. I'd like to see you in my shoes under the same conditions, among people each of whom is finer than the next. You can never get peeved at them, can never hate them, can never hold a grudge against them. And if some wild spirit got into you and you flared up at them and went home angry—all that was needed was for you to return and look them in the eye, listen to their first hello and all your anger went with the wind. In a flash, you forgot your rage and you were ready once again to go to hell and back for them. That's the sort of creatures they are. Well, what can you do? Not to mention Feygele. She was a gift of God. One look from her deep, beautiful, and nearsighted eyes was enough to drive you wild. Take it easy now, I don't mean you, I mean myself. For she drove me crazy marrying that Misha Gruzevitsh. The whole house was full of Misha. No one could eat, no one could sleep, no one could live. What was up? Misha! Misha was taken away. Misha was clapped into jail. They were going to try him. He had to be saved. But those cold-blooded characters didn't let me near him. Neither me nor her. No one. I saw that it looked bad, that the least he would get off with, if he were lucky, would be life imprisonment, if not hanging. I see you're not comfortable in this chair. Why don't you sit over here by the window? Perhaps I've bored you a bit? But it's no great tragedy. My burden is heavier than yours. It's nothing to you. You'll hear me out (I'll soon finish) and then you'll go home. But I live with this TNT forever.

Where were we? Oh yes, hanging. You've probably read in the papers that they hanged two men yesterday. Today they're hanging a few more. There's no difference nowadays between hanging people and killing chickens. And what do you do while all this is going on? You sit in your rocking chair smoking a Havana cigar, or you have yourself a snack—a fresh cup of coffee and hot buttered rolls. Do you care if they're hanging a man, who twitches and trembles during the last moments of his agony, someone you knew, one near and dear to you, someone who only yesterday was as full of life as you are now? Do you care if his warm body lies there—a body from whom the hangman has taken the life? Or if out there a man is suffering; he wants to die quickly, but he can't, for the hangman didn't tighten the noose properly or it broke and he's left dangling there, half-dead, half-alive, and with dying eyes begging the judges to render justice quickly? What's that? You can't stand that sort of talk? Are you a softie? I'm just as soft as you are. Just imagine, since I'd been everywhere, I knew the exact moment he was to be hanged. Then, I read in the papers how one of the three—they hanged all three you see—put up a struggle with death. That was Bomstein. He was heavy and so they had to hang him twice. That's how they wrote about it in the papers. And we all read it. That is, not all of us, only Rose and I. We hid the papers from the grandmother and from Feygele. That's how we added another widow to the household. Widow number three.

Grief descended upon us all—a silent, death-like grief which neither words nor colors can describe. A grief you don't dare write about, for writing about it would profane it. If one of your writers had described that grief, I would have broken his arm. It was a grief about which you could not, must not, dare not speak. We lived in memories, in the past.

Three widows—three lives. Not complete lives, but half lives. Not half lives, either—but fragments. Just the start of lives. Each had started so well, so poetically. It flashed for a moment, then was snuffed out. I'm not talking about myself. I don't count. But I see them every day, spend my evenings with them, talking of the good old days, remembering stories and events of my dear friend Pini, the kind and honest Shapiro, the hero Misha Gruzevitsh, who was written up in all the papers and described as a near-genius in the field of chemistry. Every time I leave them, I leave with heavy heart, peeved at myself. Why have I thrown away my life so foolishly, I ask myself. Where was my first mistake and what will be my last? I love all three of them. Each one of them is precious to me. Each of them might have been mine and still might be. Each one of them thinks me a dear and a bore, a necessity and a nuisance. If I don't show up one day, they're as gloomy as anything. And if I overstay a half hour, they simply show me the door. They don't take a step without consulting me. If I scold them about something, they say I'm a busybody. So I get angry and run away and lock myself up with my cat and tell the maid to tell any callers that I've gone away. Then I work at my diary, which I've been keeping for thirty-six years. It's quite an interesting book, you may be sure! I keep it for myself, only. For no one else. This literature of yours—it doesn't even deserve having a book like mine. Maybe I'll show it to you someday. But no one else. For no money in the world!

But half an hour later, there's a knocking at my door. Who is it, I want to know. "It's the maid from the widows' place. They want you to come for lunch. What should I tell her?" "Tell her I'll be right over."

Well? What have you got to say now? Where's your psychology? You're in a rush, eh? I'll join you. I have to visit my three widows. Just a minute, though. I want to leave word to feed the cat, because I'm liable to spend the whole day there. We play cards. For money! You ought to see how everyone likes to win. And if a mistake's made, we lay into each other—I into them, they into me. None of us spares the other. When someone else makes a mistake in cards, I'm liable to rip him to shreds. What's that smile on your face for? Believe me, I know what's in the back of your mind. I see right through you, but I laugh at you and your grandmother, too. You're thinking: What an old bachelor. What an old grouch!

THE PASSOVER EVE VAGABONDS

1. Kicked out of Paradise

"THANK GOD PURIM'S over and done with. Now we can start planning for Passover."

That's what Mama said the morning after Purim as she carefully inspected the four corners of the parlor like a chicken about to lay an egg. There, a few days later, we saw some hay and two boxes, upon which stood a little barrel covered by a coarse, white piece of cloth. Father and I were called into the parlor and warned about three dozen times that I not dare enter that room again, look at it from a distance, or even breathe in the general area. Immediately thereafter, the parlor door was shut, and, with all due respect, we were told to bid a hearty goodbye to the room and not set foot into it until Passover.

From that moment on, the parlor had a magnetic charm for me and I was strongly tempted to peep into that forbidden corner, if even from afar. While munching on my afternoon snack—a piece of bread smeared with chicken fat—I joyfully looked into the bright parlor. There stood the red sofa, made of the same tawny wood used for violins, the three-legged, semi-circular table, the oval, well cut mirror, and the magnificent, hand-decorated picture hanging on the east wall which faced Jerusalem. It was a work of art which Father had made when still a young man. Oh my, what *didn't* appear on it? Bears and lions, wildcats and eagles, birds and ram's horns, citrons and candelabras, the Passover plate with stars of David on it, leaves and buttons, circles, loops, and an infinite number of curlicues and dots. It was hard to believe that a human hand could have drawn all that. How talented he is, I thought. Father is perfect.

"May the devil not take you! Standing with bread at the Passover door. May you not burn in hell," Mama shouted, and with two sharp pinching fingers led me by my left ear to Father.

"Go ahead. Take a good look at your son and heir. With bread in his hands, he looked into the parlor where the Passover borscht is."

Father faked a solemn expression, shook his head, pursed his lips and clucked:

"Tsk, tsk. Off with you, you little brat."

When Mama turned to go, I noticed a sly little smile on Father's lips. As Mama faced him again, the serious look returned. He took me by the hand, put me in the adjoining chair, and told me not to look into the parlor again. It was forbidden.

"Not even from far away?" I asked.

But Father didn't hear me. He had returned to his book, deep in thought and silent study. Again I sneaked up to the parlor and peeked through a crack in the door. Before me was a Paradise of fine things: a set of brand-new crockery, shiny pots, a meat cleaver, a salting board. In addition, two ropes of onions were strung on the wall, adding charm to the room. The parlor was all set for Passover! Passover! Passover!

2. From Bad to Worse

"Perhaps I can trouble your honors to move yourselves and your books out of here and go to the big alcove?" Mama ordered.

She was dressed in white, had a white kerchief on her head, and held a long stick in one hand and a feather duster in the other. She bent her head back and looked up to the ceiling.

"Sosil. Come here with the brush! Come on, get a move on, girl. Show your face."

Sosil, the maid, a white cloth on her head too, appeared with a wet rag and a pail of whitewash. She set to work, slapping the wet brush across the ceiling, splash, splash. The two women looked like live white-shrouded corpses and both were as angry as could be.

But they didn't let me watch this rare comedy for long. First, they told me that a young boy wasn't supposed to stand and watch the ceiling being whitewashed for Passover. Then, in an angrier tone:

"Listen here! How about heading for the alcove?"

Saying this, Mama took me by the hand and showed me where to go. Since I wasn't too eager to leave, I returned and met Sosil. She pushed me away from her and said: "What a child! Always getting under your feet!"

"Go. Run off, for goodness sake. Go to your father," Mama said, and pushed me toward Sosil, who caught me and threw me back at Mama, saying: "I've never seen such a stubborn child in my life."

"He wasn't learned his lesson," Mama said and slapped my rump. Sosil grabbed me and dabbed some whitewash on my nose and I stumbled into Father's room, like a wet kitten, and burst into tears.

Father looked up from his books, tried his best to console me, put me on his lap, and started studying again.

3. From the Alcove to the Pantry

"Excuse me, boss," said Sosil to Father, "but the boss-lady told me to tell you to move to the pantry."

The maid came into the alcove armed with all her tools, painted white as a ghost. We had to pack ourselves and our books to the pantry, a place no bigger than a yawn. One bed stood there, and in it slept the maid and, to my great shame, I. Sosil, you understand, was a relative, and had been with us for many years. "When I came," she once said to me, "you weren't even born yet. You grew up under my care," she said. "If it weren't for me you'd be God knows where," she announced, "for wherever there was a tumult, a hodge-podge, a mess—you were in the midst of it and I saved you from the muddle. And that's the thanks you give me, huh?" she said, "biting the hand that fed you? Well, don't you deserve a thrashing?" she said.

That's how Sosil used to talk to me, smacking me and tugging my hair, as well. And—wonder of wonders—no one protested. Neither Father nor Mama took my part. Sosil did whatever she pleased with me. Just as if I was hers, not theirs.

I took to a corner of the pantry, sat down on the floor, looking at Father as he rubbed his forehead, chewed his beard, swayed, and sighed, "Well, that's how it is. . . ." Just then Sosil came in with her equipment and asked us to move a bit further.

"Where, now?" asked Father, completely bewildered.

"How do I know?" Sosil said, and started whitewashing the place.

"Into the little storeroom," said Mama, coming into the pantry. With her long stick and new feather-duster, she looked like a fully-armed enemy in a surprise attack.

"The storeroom is as cold as a stone." Father tried to beg his way out.

"A stone-cold plague on him," said Mama.

"Sure! They're freezing on the streets now, come spring," Sosil mocked, and started splashing her wet brush on the dry walls. We had to pick ourselves up and move to the storeroom, where we both shivered with cold. You couldn't say the place was conducive to studying. The little storeroom was narrow and dark. Two people could hardly stand there without stepping on each other's toes. But because of that, it was a miniature Paradise for me. Just imagine, there were little shelves for me to climb. But Father wouldn't let me. He said I'd fall and break my neck. But who paid any attention to him? No sooner was he into his books, than I was—yippee!—on the first, the second, the third shelf.

"Cock-a-doodle-doo!" I crowed at the top of my voice, wanting to show Father my great talent. I raised my head and before I knew it, had banged into the ceiling with such force that it practically knocked all my teeth out. Father became frightened and raised a fuss. Then Sosil, followed by Mama, came a-running, and both of them plowed into me for all they were worth.

"Did you ever see such a wild boy?" Mama asked.

"That's no boy. That's a little demon," Sosil said, adding that in a little while we'd be asked—begging our pardon a thousand times—to move ourselves to the kitchen, for most of the house was already painted-for-Passover.

4. From the Storeroom to the Kitchen

In the kitchen I saw the big-browed Moyshe-Ber sitting with Father on the dairy-bench. They weren't studying now, but pouring out their bitter hearts to each other. Father complained about his pre-Passover travels, saying, that for the past few days he'd been sent packing from one place to another. "I've become a vagabond. Gone into exile, tramping from one place to the next."

But Moyshe-Ber said, "That's nothing. I have it much worse. I've been kicked out of the house altogether."

I looked at the big-browed Moyshe-Ber and for the life of me couldn't understand how such a big Jew with such huge eyebrows could have been kicked out of his own house. Bit by bit they slipped back into their old strange talk. Maimonides, Yehuda Halevi's Kuzari, Philosophy, Spinoza, and other such nonsense which went in one ear and out the other.

The gray cat, sitting on the stove and licking its paws, was more interesting. Sosil said a cat licking herself meant a guest was coming. But I just couldn't understand how the cat knew we were going to have company. I went up to the cat and started teasing her. First, I wanted to touch her paw. But nothing doing. Then, I taught her to beg and stood her up on her hind legs. She didn't like this either. "Attention!" I told her, and slapped her nose. She closed her eyes and turned away, stuck out her tongue, and yawned as if to say: Why does this boy bother me so? What does he want of my life? But her behavior annoyed me. Why does the cat have to be such a stubborn mule, I thought, and kept teasing her until she suddenly bared her sharp claws and scratched my hand. "Mama, help," I yelled. Mama and Sosil rushed in in an uproar and I got my share of it from both of them. Next time I'd know not to fool around with cats, they said. Cats! All told there was only one little cat and they called it *cats*.

"Go wash up," Mama told Father. "We'll have our last pre-Passover meal in the cellar."

Sosil took the poker and started moving the pots around on the stove, paying no attention to either me, my father or Moyshe-Ber. Moreover, she let Moyshe-Ber know that she couldn't understand what he was doing here on the eve of Passover. That's the proper time to be home, she said, instead of lolling around in neighbors' houses. Moyshe-Ber took the hint, said goodbye, and we all went down to the cellar for our last pre-Passover meal.

5. From the Kitchen Down to the Cellar

I couldn't understand why Father made faces, shrugged his shoulders, and grumbled: "What a vagabond life!" What sort of catastrophe was it having one meal in the cellar? How could the smell of sour pickles, stinking cabbage, and crocks full of dairy products harm anyone? What was so terrible about making a table out of two upside-down barrels and a noodle-board, and using other barrels for chairs? Just the opposite. I thought it was much better that way, and more fun, too. While doing so, you could ride around the cellar on the barrel. But what if you fell? If you fell you got up and rolled around again. The only trouble was that Sosil was on a sharp lookout to foil my attempts.

"He's got himself a new game," she said. "He's dying to break a leg."

That was a lot of hooey. I no more wanted to break a leg than she did. I don't know what she wanted of me. She always picked on me and looked at the black side of things. If I ran, she said I'd break my skull. If I went near anything, she said I'd smash it. If I chewed on a button, she had a fit: "The blunderhead is going to choke himself." But I used to get even with her when I was sick. The minute I felt out of sorts, she turned the world upside-down fussing over me, and didn't know whether she was coming or going.

"Now, take the child upstairs," Mama said, after we had finished grace. "We have to clean up the last bit of leaven from the cellar too." Before Father asked her where to go, she added: "Up to the attic for a couple of hours."

"Because the floors are still wet," Sosil added quickly. "But see to it that the little bungler doesn't tumble out of the attic and break all his bones!"

"Bite your tongue!" Mama yelled, as Sosil hurried me on with a push from behind.

"Well, get a move on, bungler. Move!"

Father followed me and I heard him grumbling: "The attic! What next? There's a vagabond gypsy's life for you."

What a strange one Father was. Going up to the attic displeased him. If it were up to me, I'd like every week to be the week before Passover where I would have to climb up to the attic. First of all, the climbing itself was fun. On a regular weekday I could stretch out and die—and they wouldn't let me go up to the attic. And now I scrambled up the stairs like a little devil. Father came after me, saying, "Take it easy. Take it slowly," but who took it easy? Who took it slowly? I felt as if I'd sprouted wings and was flying, flying.

6. From the Cellar to the Attic—and that's all

You ought to see the looks of our attic. It was smack full of treasures—smashed lamps, broken pots, clothes so old you couldn't tell if they were men's or women's underwear. I found an old piece of fur there, too. As soon as I touched it, it crumbled like snow. Pages from old sacred books, the burned exhaust pipe of an old samovar, a sackful of feathers, a rusty strainer, and an old palm-branch lay on the floor, stretched out like a lord. Not to mention the planks and boards and the roof! The roof was made of pure shingle and I could touch it with my bare hands. Being able to touch the ceiling was nothing to sneeze at.

Father sat down on a cross-beam, picked up the loose pages, attached one to another, and started reading them. I stood next to the little attic window and had a picture-postcard view of all of Kasrilevke. I saw all the houses and all their roofs, black and gray, red and green. The people walking in the streets seemed tiny and I thought that ours was the finest village in the world. I peeked into our own courtyard and saw all the neighbors washing and scrubbing, scraping and rubbing, making the tables and benches kosher-for-Passover. They carried huge pots of boiling water, heated irons and red-hot bricks, all of which gave off a white vapor. It tumbled and turned until it disappeared like smoke. The smell of spring was in the air. Little streamlets flowed in the streets, goats bleated, and a man wearing cord-wrapped boots was hauling himself and a white horse through the mud. That happened to be Azriel the Wagoner. The poor devil beat his horse, who just about managed to drag his feet through the mud. He was delivering a load of matzohs to someone. Then I remembered that we had bought our matzohs a long time ago and had them locked in the cupboard over which a white sheet had been hung. In addition, we had a basketful of eggs, a jar of Passover chicken-fat, two ropes of onions on the wall, and many other delicacies for the holiday. I thought of the new clothes I'd have for Passover and my heart melted with joy.

"Boss," we heard a voice from downstairs. "Sorry to trouble you, but you'll have to come down and air out the books."

Father stood up and spat out angrily: "Damn this vagabond existence."

It was beyond me why Father wasn't happy. What could be more fun than standing outside, airing the books. I dashed from the window to the attic door, then—clompety-clomp—head-over-heels down the stairs, I went into the kitchen.

I don't know what happened next! I just know that after the fall I was ill for a long time. They tell me I almost didn't recover. But as you can see, I'm as hale and hearty as ever, may it continue that way. Except for that one scar on my face, my shortness of breath, and the constant twitch in my eyes, I'm in perfect shape.

ON AMERICA

"AMERICA IS ALL bluff. All Americans are bluffers. . . ."

That's what strangers say. Being greenhorns, they don't know what they're talking about. The fact is that America can't even shine Kasrilevke's shoes when it comes to bluffing. And our own Berel-Ayzik could put *all* the American bluffers into his side pocket.

You'll realize who Berel-Ayzik is when I tell you that if a Kasrilevkite starts jabbering a mile a minute, or as they say in America, talks himself blue in the face, he's shut up with these words: "Regards from Berel-Ayzik." He gets the hint and buttons his lip.

There's a story they tell in Kasrilevke about a fresh lout which tells a lot about Berel-Ayzik. On Easter, the Christians have a custom of greeting one another with the news that Christ is risen. The other answers by saying: True, he is risen. Well, once a Christian met up with this fresh lout of a Jew and said: "Christ is risen." The Jew felt his stomach churning. What should he do now? Saying "he is risen," would be against his belief. Saying no, he's not alive, might get him into a pickle. So he thought about it and said to the Christian: "Yes, that's what our Berel-Ayzik told us today." Just imagine, it was this very Berel-Ayzik who spent a few years in America before he returned to Kasrilevke. Picture the wonderful stories he told about that country.

"First of all—the land itself. A land flowing with milk and honey. People make money left and right. Beggars use two hands. They rake it in. And there's so much business there, it makes you dizzy. You do whatever you please. Want a factory—it's a factory. Want to open a store—fine. Want to push a pushcart, that's permitted, too. Or you can become a pedlar, even work in a shop! It's a free country. You can swell from hunger, die in the street, and no one'll bother you, no one'll say a word.

"As for its size. The width of its streets! The height of its buildings! They have a structure called the Woolworth building. Its tip scratches the clouds and then some. They say it has several hundred floors. How do you get to the top? With a ladder called an elevator. To get to the top floor, you board the elevator early in the morning and you reach your floor by sunset.

"Once I wanted to find out, just for the fun of it, what it looked like up there, and I'm not sorry I went. What I saw, I'll never see again. What I felt up there cannot even be described. Just imagine, I stood at the top and looked down. Suddenly I felt a queer kind of smooth and icy cold on my left cheek. Not so much like ice as jello, slippery and nappy-like. Slowly I turned to my left and looked—it was the moon.

"And their way of life. It's all rush and panic, hustle and bustle. Hurry-up is what they call it. They do everything quickly. They even rush when they eat. They dash into a restaurant and order a glass of whiskey. I myself saw a man being served a plate which had something fresh and quivering on it. As the man lifted his knife, half of it flew off to one side, half to the other, and that put an end to that man's lunch.

"But you ought to see how healthy they are. Men as strong as steel. They have a habit of fighting in the middle of the street. Not that they want to kill you, knock your eye out, or push a few teeth down your throat like they do here. God forbid! They fight just for fun. They roll up their sleeves and slug away to see who beats who. Boxing is what they call it. One day, while carrying some merchandise, I took a walk in the Bronx. Suddenly two young boys started up with me. They wanted to box. "No, sir," I said. "I don't box." Well, we argued back and forth, but they wouldn't let me leave. I thought it over: if that's the way you feel about it, I'll show you a thing or two. I put my package down, took off my coat, and they beat the daylights out of me. I made it away, my life hanging by a hair. Since then, all the money in the world won't get me to box.

"Not to mention the respect we Jews have there. No people are as honored and exalted there as the Jew. A Jew's a big shot there. It's a mark of distinction to be a Jew. On *Sukkoth* you can meet Jews carrying citrons and palm-branches even on Fifth Avenue. And they're not even afraid of being arrested. If I tell you that they love Jews it has nothing to do with the fact that they hate a Jewish beard and earlocks. Whiskers are what they call them. If they see a Jew with whiskers, they leave the Jew alone, but tug away at his whiskers until he has to snip them off. That's why most of the Jews don't wear beards or earlocks. Their faces are as smooth as glass. It's hard to tell who's a Jew and who isn't. You can't tell by the beard and by the language, but at least you can recognize him by his hurried walk and by his hands when he talks. But aside from that, they're Jews down to the last drop. They observe all the Jewish customs, love all Jewish foods, celebrate all the Jewish holidays. Passover is Passover! Matzohs are baked all year round. And there's even a separate factory for the bitter herbs we use during that holiday. Thousands upon thousands of workers sit in that factory and make bitter herbs. And they even make a living from it. America's nothing to sneeze at!"

"Yes, Berel-Ayzik, what you say is all very well and good. But just tell us one more thing. Do they die in America like they do here? Or do they live forever?"

"Of course they die! Why shouldn't they die? When they drop dead in America, they drop dead by the thousands each day. Ten and twenty thousands. Even thirty thousand. They drop dead by the streetful. Entire cities get swallowed up like Korah in the Bible. They just sink right into the ground and disappear. America's nothing to sneeze at."

"Then what's the big deal with Americans? In other words, they die like us."

"As for dying, sure they die. But it's *how* you die—that's the thing. Dying is the same all over. It's death that kills them. The main thing is the burial. That's it! First of all, in America it's customary to know where you're going to be buried. The man himself, while he's still alive, goes to the cemetery and picks out his own plot. He bargains for it until the price suits him. Then he takes his wife, goes out to the cemetery, and says: "See, dear? That's where you'll be. That's where I'll be. That's where our children'll be." The next thing he does is go to the funeral office and order whichever class funeral he wants. They come in three classes—first, second, and third. The first-class affair is for the real rich men, millionaires. It costs a thousand dollars. That's what I call a funeral! The sun shines, the weather is lovely. The coffin lies on a black, silver-plated catafalque. The horses wear black harnesses and white plumes. The rabbis and cantors and sextons are dressed in white-buttoned, black outfits. Carriages follow the coffin—carriages without end. All the children of all the Hebrew schools assemble at one point and they slowly sing the verse from the Psalms: "Righteousness shall go before him and shall set his steps on the way." This chant makes the town's rafters ring. It's no trifle! A thousand dollars!

"The second-class funeral is quite nice, too. It only costs five hundred dollars, but can't compete with the first-class affair. The weather isn't too peachy. The coffin lies on a black catafalque, but it isn't silver-plated. The horses and the rabbis are dressed in black—no plumes, no buttons. Carriages follow, but not as many as in the first-class affair. Children come, but only from a few Hebrew schools and they don't stretch the verse out as much. "Righteousness shall go before him and shall set his steps on the way." They use the mournful Psalms melody as befits the five hundred dollar rate.

"The third-class funeral is a shabby one and costs only a hundred dollars. The weather is cold and foggy. The coffin has no catafalque. There are two horses and two reverends. Not a carriage in sight. The children from one Hebrew school dash off their line without a tune. They mumble it so sleepily you can hardly hear them. After all, it only costs a hundred dollars. What can you expect for a hundred dollars?"

"Yes, but what happens, Berel-Ayzik, to a man who doesn't even have the hundred?"

"He's in hot water. Without money, it's bad all over. The pauper is half dead and buried anyway. But don't get any wrong ideas. Even in America they don't let the poor man lie around unburied. They give him a free funeral. It doesn't even cost him a penny. It's a pathetic funeral, to be sure. There's no ceremony whatever. There's no hint of a horse or a reverend. It rains cats and dogs. Only two sextons come, the first sexton on one side, the second on the other, and in the middle, the corpse himself. Then all three drag their feet over to the cemetery. It's hell being born without money. It's a lousy world . . . ! By the way, can anybody here spare an extra cigarette?"

75,000

Troubles, you say? You call *everything* troubles. But *I* think that since the beginning of time and the creation of the Jewish people, a trouble like mine hasn't been heard, felt, or seen even in the wildest dream. If you have the time, move up a bit, pay close attention, and I'll tell you the story of 75,000 from *a* to *z*, down to the very last detail.

The whole affair makes my chest tighten; it gags me; it sends a stream of fire through me. I feel that I *must* get it out of my system. You get the picture? Just do me one favor. If I interrupt my story or get sidetracked and start jabbering about Boyberik, just lead me back to it. Ever since this business of the 75,000, you see, my ears have been ringing— and I usually forget where I'm at. I don't wish the likes of it on you! You get the picture? By the way, can you spare 75,000—damn it—I mean, a cigarette?

Well then, where was I? Oh, yes, the 75,000. . . . You're looking at a man whose lottery ticket won the 75,000 rubles this past May 1. At first you might think: well what's there to listen to? Don't plenty of people win money? Don't folks say that a man from Nikolay won two hundred thousand and a young bookkeeper from Odessa forty thousand rubles? But not a peep is heard from them. Everything is fine and dandy. True, right, everyone expects the big prizes. One hundred thirty-six million people envy us. You get the picture? But the point is, there's no comparing one prize and another. The story of *this* prize is an amazing one which weaves into, around, and out of itself. You really have to prop yourself up and hear me out to the end to understand what's going on.

First of all, let me introduce myself. I'm not going to give you a song and dance that I'm a great scholar, philosopher, or man of wealth. You're looking at a plain, down-to-earth Jew who has his own house and a respected name in town, as well. You get the picture? True, I once had money, lots of it. Then again, how can I say lots? Certainly Brodsky had much more. But, in any case, I did have a few thousand rubles. Then, God took pity on me, as they say, and I was bitten by the bug-to-get-rich-quick. I started selling wheat in the famine-stricken districts and was left flat broke. But at least I could still meet my debts. No doubt you think that as soon as I lost the money I became depressed. Well then, you don't know me. Money means no more to me than—I don't know—a cigarette butt! It means absolutely nothing to me. How do I mean nothing? Sure, money is important, but to go fight over it, or kill yourself for it—not on your life! When you don't have what you need, if you can't live properly, if you can't give the donation you'd like to give—*then* things are bad. Take my word for it—when they ask one villager for a three-ruble contribution for the communal funds and skip *me*, it annoys the daylights out of me. You get the picture? I'd rather get hell from my wife as to why there's no money for Sabbath provisions than say no to a poor man while I still have forty kopeks jangling in my pocket. You get the picture? That's the sort of madman I am. By the way, do you have forty . . . damn it . . . I mean a match?

Well then, where was I? Oh, yes, the rubles. I lost the few rubles and was left without a kopek to my name. Having lost my few rubles and being left without a kopek to my name, I told my wife one fine morning:

"Tsipora, listen to what I've got to say. We're clean broke."

"What do you mean by clean broke?" she said.

"We don't even have a kopek to our name."

Well, being a female, she immediately started bawling. "Oh, my God. We're sunk. We're lost. We're six feet under. What are you talking about Yakov-Yosil—where's all your money?"

"Shush up! Pipe down! What are you raising such a racket for? Who says it was my money? God gave and God took. Or like they say: Ivan never had and never will have money. Who says that Yakov-Yosil is supposed to have two maids, a four-room apartment and wear a silken Sabbath cloak? There's plenty of Jews who are starving. But do they die? If you keep asking why this, why that, the world wouldn't exist for long."

I cited other examples and proverbs and my wife finally admitted that I was right. You get the picture? You ought to know that I'm married to a woman I'm proud of. She has a good head on her shoulders. You don't have to plead too long to make your point. She stopped her sniffling and fussing immediately and even took to consoling me, saying that the whole thing was probably fated, that God is a merciful Father and would watch over us. . . .

Without dilly-dallying, I sub-leased my apartment, moved into one tiny room and kitchen, and, begging your pardon, dismissed the maids. My wife, may she live and be well, rolled up her sleeves and became the cook. And I let it be known that I, Reb Yakov-Yosil, was to be called Pauper. What do I mean by Pauper? As you can well imagine, there are plenty poorer than me. After all, I still had an apartment, a piece of property from which I could make my livelihood. The only trouble was that there were four weeks in the month. Had there been only two weeks in a month, maybe our expenses and income would have balanced. Each month always had two extra weeks and, naturally, that's no good. But, never mind. Like they say—you get used to troubles. Let me tell you, being a poor man is the most peaceful thing in the world. Your mind is free of headaches, payments, loans, rat-races, and a topsy-turvy world. But wait—there's a God up above who says: What good is it, Yakov-Yosil, having peace of mind and living without troubles? Do you have a ticket to the lottery? Well, here's 75,000 for you, go break your neck with it! You get the picture? By the way, do you happen to have a ticket—damn it—I mean, a cigarette?

Well then, where was I? Oh, yes, the lottery ticket. Ticket? You think it's so simple for a Jew to have a ticket and collect the 75,000? Wait just a minute. First of all, why does a Jew have a ticket? So that he can pawn it and get some money for it. Well then, why don't you go into a bank, Yakov-Yosil, you ass, and get some cash for it? But the excuses are that in the first place there are no banks in our village and, secondly, what do I need the bank for? Can't a bank go bankrupt if it has a mind to? Then again, things do operate in an orderly manner in this orderly world and no one was grabbing the ticket out of my hand. Who wanted my ticket anyway? You get the picture? Well, that's what I thought at the time. On second thought, perhaps I didn't really think at all. But I decided: my tenant, a fine young man, a gentleman and a scholar, was a money-lender. Why not pawn the ticket with him? If he'd give me 200 for it, I'd take it. Why shouldn't I? So I went over to him—Birnbaum, he was called—and said:

"Mr. Birnbaum, would you give me 200 rubles for my ticket?"

"I'll give you 200 rubles for your ticket," he said.

"How much interest would I have to pay?" I said.

"How much interest do you want me to charge you?" he said.

"How do I know?" I said. "Charge me bank rates."

"I'll charge you bank rates," he said.

In a nutshell, we settled on the interest, I pawned my ticket for five months, and took the 200 rubles. You get the picture? Then why don't you take a receipt from him, Yakov-Yosil, you ass, stating that you left such-and-such a ticket of series and number so-and-so. But, no! Just the opposite. Birnbaum took a receipt from *me* that I borrowed 200 rubles for five months and left him such-and-such a ticket of series and number so-and-so. And if I didn't pay the 200 rubles in time, said ticket would be his and I would have nothing on him. You get the picture? You know what I thought then? I thought: what's there to be afraid of? In any case, if I'd redeem the ticket at the proper time and pay my debt, everything would be fine and dandy. If not, I'd pay him the interest due and he'd just have to wait. Why wouldn't he wait? Why should he care, so long as he got the interest? You get the picture? Well, here's what happened. When the time came, naturally, I didn't redeem the ticket. Five months passed, then another five. Slowly it stretched on into two years and five months. I kept paying the interest, of course. That is, sometimes I paid, sometimes not. What was I afraid of? Would he sell the ticket? He wouldn't sell my ticket. Why should he sell my ticket? Anyway, that's what I thought at the time. On second thought, perhaps I really didn't think at all. Meanwhile, times were bad, business was rotten; the extra weeks in the months kept piling up and I worked my fingers to the bone. What was one to do? Just live and be well—there were always plenty of troubles! And this situation lasted until Passover.

But this year, before Passover, God sent a little business my way. I bought a few carloads of millet. The price of millet skyrocketed. I sold the millet and, thank heaven, made a neat profit on the millet. I had myself a Passover that Brodsky himself would have envied. Not owing a kopek to a soul and having a few hundred rubles to your name to boot was nothing to sneeze at. I was riding high—you get the picture? So why don't you take two hundred rubles, Yakov-Yosil, you ass, and pay Birnbaum and buy back your lottery ticket? But, no. I decided—what's the rush? He won't run away with the ticket. After Passover will be time enough. If not, I'll pay the interest and take a receipt for the ticket. Anyway, that's what I thought then. On second thought, perhaps I didn't really think at all. You get the picture? I upped and turned the money into sacks which I stored in a warehouse. Well, thank goodness for a miracle—the lock was jimmied that night. It happened right after Passover, on April 30, the night before the May 1 lottery drawing. All my sacks were stolen! I was flat broke again.

"Tsipora," I said to my wife. "You know what? We're flat broke again."

"What do you mean flat broke?"

"We don't even have a *sack* to our name," I said.

"What do you mean? Where did the sacks disappear to?"

"They've been carried off! Right out of the warehouse!"

Being a woman, naturally, she started bawling and wailing.

"Shush up, Tsipora," I said. "Don't yell. You're not alone here. Make believe the house burned down and we got out of it naked as the day we were born. Does that make you feel any better?"

"What a comparison?" she said. "Is that why they have to steal your sacks?"

"What's one thing got to do with the other?" I said. "Mark my words, the sacks will be found."

"How are they going to get to you?" she said. "Are the crooks going to present you with the sacks just because you're called Yakov-Yosil? They don't have anything better to do, eh?"

"Go on!" I said. "You're a ninny. Man can't even imagine the wonders of God!"

Well, here's what happened! The sacks, of course, were goners. What sacks? Where sacks? But I ran around like a madman, contacted the police, searched high and low, poked into every rat-hole. But it was a lost cause. Like trying to find yesterday. You get the picture? My head was in another world, my heart was in my throat, my mouth was dry— I was completely depressed. But around noon, while standing near the local stock exchange, that is, near the pharmacy on the marketplace, a thought flew through my mind: after all, today's some sort of judgment day. The lottery drawing—the first of May. God can do anything! We have an Almighty God. If only He wills it, He can make me and my whole family happy.

Then, remembering the stolen sacks, I forgot all about the first of May lottery drawing and started looking for the sacks again. I had a little clue and kept searching the whole day into the rest of that night and on until the dawn of May 2. I was in a complete daze, I hadn't eaten for twenty-four hours and here it was 1 P.M. and I was passing out. You get the picture?

When I came home, my wife pounced on me: "How about washing up and having a bite? Haven't you had enough of that sack affair. Your sacks are sticking like a bone in my throat. The devil take those sacks. Do you have to kill yourself on account of those sacks? We'll be no better off with or without the sacks. What a business with sacks! Here sacks, there sacks. All I hear is sacks, sacks, sacks."

"You know, wife, dear?" I said. "Let's forget about the sacks, huh? I've been sacked enough as is. Now *you* come along and rub salt into my wounds. Sacks, sacks, sacks." You get the picture? Can I trouble you for a sack—damn it—I mean, another cigarette?

Well then, where was I? Oh yes, the sacks. Well, it was a lost cause. What to do? I wasn't going to kill myself for them. I washed and sat down to eat, but—nothing doing! My appetite was gone.

"What's wrong with you, Yakov-Yosil?" asked my wife, God bless her. "Who crossed you today?"

"I myself don't know what the matter is," I said, left the table in the middle of the meal, and lay down on the sofa. No sooner did I stretch out than the paper was delivered. Why then don't you take it, Yakov-Yosil, you ass, and see if perhaps your ticket won a prize? After all, it *is*

May 2d. But no go. I didn't know if it was the second of May, the twenty-first of June, or the Ides of March Slave. You get the picture? Well then, I picked up the paper and started reading it like the prayer book—from the very beginning. The long and the short of it was that I lay there reading all sorts of news. Shootings and hanging, stabbings and murders. The English and the Boers. Naturally, it all went in one ear and out the other. Who gave a damn about the English and the Boers when my sacks were gone! The whole pack of them weren't worth one of my stolen sacks. Anyway, that's what I thought at the time. But on second thought, perhaps I really didn't think at all. I flipped from one page to the next, scanning, and then I saw—LOTTERY DRAW-ING. Suddenly a thought hit me. Perhaps my ticket has won 500 rubles at least. That would be a handy heaven-sent substitute for my sacks. I went through the list of winners of 500 rubles. Nothing. The 1,000 ruble section. Nothing. Certainly not 5, 8, or 10,000. I kept this up until I got to the 75,000 listing. As I looked at that number, I saw stars and felt a violent pounding in my head. Series 2289, number 12. I could have sworn it was my number. But then again, how does a bun-gler like me come to such a big prize? I took a long look at the num-bers and—great God!—it was my number. I wanted to rise from the sofa—but couldn't. I was glued to it. I wanted to call "Tsipora"—but couldn't. My tongue was stuck to my palate. Mustering all my strength, I got up, went to my desk, and looked at my note book. As I lived and breathed—series 2289, number 12.

"Tsipora," I said, my hands shaking, my teeth chattering. "Know what? The stolen sacks have been found."

She looked at me as if I were crazy.

"What are you talking about. Do you know what you're saying?"

"I'm just trying to tell you," I said, "that God has paid us back for our sacks a thousand-fold and then some. Our ticket has been picked and we've won a barrelful of cash."

"Are you serious, Yakov-Yosil, or are you teasing?"

"Teasing?" I said. "I'm quite serious. We ought to be congratulated. We've won money."

"How much have we won?" she said, looking me straight in the eye, as if to say: if you're lying, better watch out!

"Well, for example, how much do you think we've won?"

"How do I know?" she said. "Probably a few hundred rubles."

"Why not a few thousand?" I said.

"How much is a few thousand?" she said. "Five? Six? Or perhaps all of seven?"

"You can't think of anything higher, can you?"

"Ten thousand?"

"Use your head," I said. "More."

"Fifteen thousand?"

"More."

"Twenty, twenty-five?"

"More!"

"Tell me, Yakov-Yosil, don't tease me!"

"Tsipora," I said, taking her hand and squeezing it. "We've won a gold mine. We're in the chips. You've never even dreamed of the amount we've won!"

"Well, tell me how much we've won, Yakov-Yosil, don't keep me in suspense!"

"We've won a load of money," I said, "a treasure-chest, a grand total of 75,000 rubles. You hear, Tsipora? 75,000!"

"God be praised," she said, and started running around the room, wringing her hands. "May your name be blessed for looking down upon us, too, and making us happy. Thank you, dear God, thank you. Are you sure, Yakov-Yosil? Is there no error, heaven forbid? Praised is your name, dear God, true and merciful Father! The whole family will be over-joyed, our good friends will be happy, our enemies will eat their hearts out. Such a load of money, knock wood, is nothing to sneeze at. How much did you say, Yakov-Yosil, 75,000?"

"75,000," I said. "Give me my coat, Tsipora, and I'll be on my way."

"Where are you off to?"

"What do you mean, where? I have to step into Birnbaum's place. That's where I've pawned my lottery ticket. And I don't even have a re-ceipt for it."

As soon as she heard these words, she turned all colors, grabbed both my hands and said, "Yakov-Yosil, in God's name, don't go now. Think it over first. Think of what you're doing, where you're going and what you're going to say. Don't forget, it's 75,000!"

"You're talking like a fishwife," I said. "So what if it's 75,000. Am I a child?"

"Listen to me, Yakov-Yosil," she said. "Think it over first. Consult a good friend. Don't go there right now. I won't let you."

To make a long story short, you know quite well that when a woman puts her foot down, she wins. We called in a good friend and told him the whole story. Having heard us out, he said that my wife was right, for 75,000 was no trifle; in the meantime, someone else had my ticket and I had no receipt for it; money was tempting and who knows what evil thoughts might come to him. After all, it was 75,000.

You get the picture? Well, how shall I put it? The both of them put me into such a blue funk that I myself became frightened and started suspecting God knows what. How should I handle the situation? We

decided that I take 200 rubles (cash was to be had at a moment's notice—a prize winner was good security), plus another man who would
stand outside the door while I spoke to Birnbaum, paid him my debt
and the interest, and bought back my ticket. In any case, if he gave back
the ticket—fine. If not, I would at least have a witness. You get the picture? But all this would be grand, I thought, if he still didn't know that
the ticket had won the 75,000. But what to do if he too had a paper and
noticed the winning number? What would I do if he'd say: "First of all,
I returned the ticket a long time ago. Second of all, that's not the number you gave me, and third of all, you never gave me a ticket at all." You
get the picture? Unless, of course, miraculously, he hadn't as yet heard
about the prize.

"Remember now, Yakov-Yosil, it's no trifle. You're going for 75,000.
Don't let them see a hint or a trace of that 75,000 on your face. But no
matter what happens, remember that your life is worth 75 times 75,000."

Those were my wife's words, God bless her. She took me by the
hands and asked me to give her my word, my word of honor, that I'd remain calm. Calm? How could I be calm when my heart was pounding
away and my thoughts buzzed a mile a minute. I couldn't forgive myself. Yakov-Yosil, you ass, how could you give Birnbaum, a complete
stranger, a ticket worth 75,000, and not even take a receipt or say a
word. By the way, do you have a word—damn it,—I mean, a cigarette?

Well then, where was I? Oh yes, Birnbaum. I would be in a pretty
pickle, I thought, if Birnbaum had read the paper and already learned
of the 75,000, perhaps even before I did. Then I would come up to him
and say: "God be with you, Mr. Birnbaum."

"Greetings," he would say. "What's the good word?"

"Where's my ticket?" I would say.

"What ticket?" he would say.

"The ticket of series 2289, number 12, which I've pawned with you."
He would look at me, wide-eyed and innocent.

Thoughts like these flashed through my mind. I felt my chest tightening; I had a choking sensation in my throat; I couldn't catch my
breath. But what was the upshot? I came to Birnbaum's house and
asked where he was. Sleeping, they told me. Sleeping? An excellent
sign that he doesn't suspect a thing. Blessed are you, dear God! I entered the house and met his wife, Feygele, in the kitchen. It was hot,
smoky, and knee-deep in filth.

"Reb Yakov-Yosil! Welcome! What a surprise!" said Feygele. She invited me in, seated me at the head of the table, and asked why haven't
I come around.

"How do I know why? I don't know myself," I said, looking her
straight in the eye, thinking: "Does she know or doesn't she know."

"Well, what are you doing, Reb Yakov-Yosil?"

"What should I be doing?" I said. "You've probably heard about my bundle of troubles."

"What troubles?"

"What?" I said. "Haven't you heard about the affair of the stolen sacks?"

"Is *that* all?" she said. "That's an old story by now. I thought it was something new."

"Something new? Was it the 75,000 she meant? I thought, and looked into her eyes. But they told me absolutely nothing.

"How about having a glass of tea, Reb Yakov-Yosil, until my husband gets up. I'll have the samovar heated."

"A glass of tea? Sure. Why not?" I said. But my heart thumped, I couldn't catch my breath, my mouth was dry, the room was hot, I was sweating, Feygele was chattering away and for the life of me I didn't know what the devil she was talking about. My head, you see, was in that little room where Birnbaum slept, snoring away so lustily. You get the picture?

"Why aren't you drinking?" said Feygele.

"What then am I doing?" I said, and kept stirring the spoon in the glass.

"You've been playing with the spoon for an hour," she said, "and you haven't even taken a sip."

"Thanks," I said. "I don't drink cold—I mean, hot tea. I like the tea to stand a while and get good and hot . . . I mean, good and cold. What I mean to say is, I like the tea to heat up, I mean cool off."

"You seem to be in a complete dither, Reb Yakov-Yosil," she said. "You're in such a daze, you don't know what you're saying. Is that what the stolen sacks have done to you? With God's help, the sacks will be found. I heard they found a clue. Wait, there's my husband, stirring. He's getting up now. Here he comes."

Birnbaum appeared, wearing a silk skullcap. He was still sleepy and rubbed his eyes, looking at me out of the corner of his eye.

"How are you, Reb Yakov-Yosil?"

My first thought was—does he know or doesn't he? At first, it seemed that he did not know. Then again, perhaps he did.

"How do you expect me to be?" I said. "You heard about my bad luck with the sacks."

"That incident has whiskers already. Tell us something new. Feygele, how about some jam? Sleep has left a funny taste in my mouth," Birnbaum said, making a face.

Well, so long as he was asking for jam, it was a good sign that he knew nothing, I thought. We started a conversation about . . . the devil knows what! It made no sense at all. My stomach was churning; I was gagging; I felt as if I were passing out. In another minute I'd topple over and start yelling: "Help, fellow Jews, it's 75,000!" You get the picture? Finally, with the good Lord's help, I brought up the subject of interest.

"I can give you some of the interest, Mr. Birnbaum," I said, "that is, I can pay up the entire interest for the ticket."

"With pleasure," he said, tasting a spoonful of jam, "with all due respect, why not?"

"How much do I owe you?"

"Do you want to know what's coming to me, or do you really want to pay cash?"

"No, no," I said. "I mean cash."

"Feygele," he called, "bring the account book over."

Hearing these words, I felt as if I'd come back from the dead. Poor chap, he didn't know the first thing about the prize.

After paying the interest, I told him: "Excuse me, Mr. Birnbaum, but note in your book that you got the interest for the ticket of series 2289, number 12."

"Feygele," he said, "note that it was paid for ticket series 2289, number 12."

He doesn't know a thing, I thought, and started talking about the ticket: it didn't pay to own one and have to pay interest on it. Then I asked: "What will become of the ticket?"

"Why bring it up now?" he asked, staring at me out of the corner of his eye.

That look made my heart leap. I didn't like the looks of that look. You get the picture? But I covered up immediately and said:

"I mentioned it because the ticket's costing me an arm and a leg. I swear, you ought to extend the loan and take 1 per cent less. Like they say—for friendship's sake."

"No," he said. "Anything else, yes, but this—no. If you want it under the old terms, fine. If not, pay me my money and pawn your ticket elsewhere."

"Even now?" I asked and my heart hammered away within me; rappety-rap, rappety-rap.

"This very minute," he said.

"Here's your money," I said, taking out the 200 rubles, my heart in my mouth.

"Take the money," he said to Feygele, bending over his tea and tasting a spoonful of jam. This was followed by another spoonful, and then a third, a fourth, a fifth. I was dying to get hold of my lottery ticket, and here he was eating jam. Every wasted moment was costing me my health. But you can't be a glutton about it. If he liked jam, let him enjoy it. It wasn't proper to drive someone by the scuff of his neck. So I had to sit and nurse my bleeding heart until he'd put an end to that jam-gobbling. You get the picture? Do you happen to have some jam . . . damn it . . . I mean a cigarette?

Well then, where was I? Oh, yes, Birnbaum eating jam. Having finished, he wiped his lips and said: "Reb Yakov-Yosil, I've taken the money. I've been paid the interest, and now I have to give you the ticket, right?"

"Seems fair," I said, faking a nonchalant expression. But I nearly dropped dead out of sheer joy.

"There's only one hitch," he said. "I can't give you the ticket today."

As soon as he said this I felt something tearing in my heart. I came down from seventh heaven back to earth. I don't know what kept me on my feet.

"What's wrong, Mr. Birnbaum?" I asked, "why can't you give me the ticket?"

"Because I don't have it here."

"What do you mean, you don't have it here?"

"It's at the bank."

Hearing this, I felt better and fell into a deep thought.

"What are you thinking about?"

"Nothing special. I was just wondering how I and the ticket'll get together."

"Simple," he said. "Tomorrow I'll go into town and bring it to you."

"Fine," I stood, said goodbye, made a motion for the door, but immediately turned back.

"How do you like that? What a businessman I am! I've returned your money, paid the interest, but you still have the ticket. At least give me a receipt for it."

"What good will a receipt do you?" he asked. "Don't you trust me for 200 rubles without a receipt?"

"Perhaps you're right," I said, heading back to the door. Then I turned around again and added: "No. It isn't right. It isn't business-like. If someone else has your ticket, you should have a receipt for it. Listen to me, Mr. Birnbaum—give me a receipt. Why not give me a receipt?"

Suddenly Birnbaum picked himself up and went back to his little curtained-off room and called his wife.

"Mr. Birnbaum," I shouted, "I know why you've called Feygele. You're going to tell her to send the maid out for the paper. Since today's the second of May you want to look and see if your ticket's won any money. But why bother? *I'll* tell you the news. My ticket, thank God, has won prize money."

Birnbaum turned all colors.

"Is that so?" he said. "May God be with you. How much did the ticket win?"

"The ticket has struck gold," I said, "may all Jews have like luck. And that's why I want a receipt from you, you get the picture?"

"As I said before, may God grant you the entire 200,000," he said. "From the bottom of my heart, believe me, I don't begrudge it to you. Come on now, how much did the ticket bring in? Don't be afraid to say it."

"Mr. Birnbaum," I said, "why drag it out and why beat around the bush? The ticket has won 75,000—you have the ticket, the interest is paid, the capital I've returned, and now give me my ticket. But you say you don't have it, that it's in the bank. Then hand over a receipt and let's get this affair over with."

It was no use. A wild look came into Birnbaum's eyes; his face became inflamed. Seeing that he was in a bad way, I took him aside and held his hands.

"Dear friend. Have pity on me and on yourself. Tell me what you want. We'll come to an understanding. But don't torment me. I can hardly stand on my feet as it is. Tell me how much you want and give me a receipt for the ticket. It's no use—I won't leave without a receipt, for it's a question of 75,000 rubles."

"What do you want me to say?" he said, his eyes blazing. "We'll let people mediate. Whatever they say, we'll do."

"What do you want other people for?" I said. "Let's be people ourselves. In the name of God, Birnbaum, listen to me. How much do you want? Let's not have it come to ridicule and scandal."

"Only mediation!" he said. "Whatever they say, I'll do."

Seeing that it would do no good, I opened the door and told my witness: "Zeydl. You can go now!" Zeydl took off like a bat out of hell and spread the news all over town: Yakov-Yosil's lottery ticket had won 75,000 rubles and Birnbaum had it and wouldn't give it back. You get the picture? That's all they needed. A half hour later, Birnbaum's place was packed, and the street was filled with a tumultuous crowd, yelling on top of their voices.

"Ticket!"

"Yakov-Yosil!"

"Birnbaum!"

"75,000."

The crowd sided with me. Some banged on the table, others promised to beat the daylights out of Birnbaum and smash his house to bits. And they weren't kidding either. But the upshot was, we'd let the town's rich man decide. Whatever he'd say would be done. The entire kit and kaboodle went over to his place.

You ought to know that our town's rich man is a soft-spoken, decent, and honest gentleman. He hates all this mediation business. But, since the whole pack of us swooped down on his home, shouting, "Save us"—for, if not, they'd tear the place apart—he had no choice but to take on the burden. We promised that his decision would be final, and poor Birnbaum had to sign the ticket over to the rich man. We all agreed to go into town, either the next day or the day after that, God willing, and take the ticket out of the bank. I would pay Birnbaum whatever sum the rich man ordered. You get the picture? Now you probably think that that finished it. Tsk, tsk, tsk. The fun's just beginning. You see, I had a partner to the ticket. Did you ever know a Jew who owned a ticket outright? Who was my partner? My partner happened to be my own brother, Henikh, who lived in a small village not far from here. It was because of *him*, really, that I pawned the ticket with Birnbaum. I mean, just the reverse, that is, it was because of *me* that my brother had the ticket pawned by Birnbaum. You get the picture? But there's a long story that goes with it, which I must tell you from *a* to *z* to make it clear.

Well then, where was I? Oh, yes, my brother Henikh. Well, I have a brother Henikh—may he live to be a hundred and twenty—what can I say? It isn't right to talk about your own brother, is it? It's like cutting your nose to spite your face. But, never mind. Don't ask! My brother and I don't think much of each other, you get the picture? May God repay me for all the things I've done for him. I can well boast that I set him on his feet. Save God alone, I'm the one who made a man out of him. But I don't have to impress you! You get the picture? So, when he sends me a lottery ticket and asks me to either sell it or pawn it for 200 rubles and send him the money—you'd think I've got the right and privilege to do so, eh? But once that was done, do you think he gave a damn about the ticket? Do you think he ever gave it a second thought? *I* took care of it, *I* insured it, *I* paid the interest on it. What did he care? And when with God's help the ticket won a prize, who beat his head against the wall with Birnbaum? Who almost got apoplexy before a way out of the dilemma was found? Finally, when we got down to brass tacks, my brother argued:

"Who asked you to drop dead for my ticket?"

Well, did you ever? How's that for gall? I tell you, this boorish attitude peeved me no end.

"Since you're such a low-down ass, who says the ticket is yours?" I said.

"Then whose is it?"

"Whose ever it is, it is," I said. "But in the meantime, we have to get it out of strange hands. Seventy-five thousand rubles is no trifle, you know."

You get the picture?

Well, how was I repaid? With scandal! With him banging on tables and smashing my chairs. Listen, if the whole world and his brother says you can't make a skullcap out of a sow's ear, they're probably right. Why fight with my brother for nothing, I decided. One hundred thirty-six million envy our prize and we brothers, sons of one mother and father, end up squabbling over it. My ticket, your ticket—phoo! It was a damn shame. Our first move was to redeem the ticket. That was prefer-able to all else, right? But go argue with an ignoramus. I'm referring to my own brother, Henikh, may God not punish me for these words. Had he only told me beforehand what was eating him—that the ticket wasn't like all others, that there was a snag in the proceedings—I would have known what to do! But when do you think he mentioned the snag? Way, way later, when the ticket had long been signed over to the rich man and the judge had, begging your pardon, impounded the ticket in the bank, called for an investigation, that is, summoned each of us to give him all the facts about the ticket.

"How did you get this ticket?" he asked me. "What connection has Birnbaum with it? And how does the rich man fit in?"

Believe me, it was some to-do, you get the picture? What has the judge got to do with us? Why does he have to know all these stories? But listen, here's where the real snag begins—the sort of snag one can-not get out of. Like a bone stuck in your throat which won't go up or down. It just chokes you. Do you want to know the source of that snag? It originated with some sort of a priest, a monk. You get the picture? There was this monk in my brother's village with whom Henikh had dealings for many years. On his word alone, he used to borrow money from the monk and sell him merchandise. They got along like friends. You get the picture?

But then something happened. According to the monk—and go be-lieve him and his word of honor—my brother came to him one day and said: "Father, I need a small loan, 200 rubles. I have to go to the fair."

"How can I give you something I don't have?" the monk said.

"That's no excuse," said my brother. "I need the 200 badly."

"What a queer Jew you are," the monk said. "I tell you, I have no money. But, if you wish, I can lend you a lottery ticket for which you might get some money."

"You get the picture? That's the very same ticket which won the 75,000. Anyway, that's what the monk said, and go believe him and his word of honor. Now that the ticket won the prize, the monk naturally came running to my brother and said: "The ticket has won a neat prize, thank God."

"That's what they say," my brother said.

"Well, what'll happen?" said the monk.

"Well, what do you expect to happen?" my brother said.

To make a long story short, they argued back and forth. One said this, the other that. One said cheese, the other, beans. But neither of them had anything signed in black and white. You get the picture? Then again, my brother, at any rate, had the ticket. But what did the monk have? Aggravation! The upshot was, the monk begged Henikh to give him at least a few thousand rubles. Then why don't you button his lip with a couple of thousand rubles, you mangy lout, and let him stop pestering you?

"He doesn't have it coming to him," my brother argued. "It's my ticket. May I drop dead if I didn't buy that ticket from him three years ago."

Well, that might have been the end of it. But you know our Jews, God bless them. The village itself is oh such a fine one. Perhaps you've heard of it. Naginsk, it's called, and like its name it's full of nags and tattle-tales, may it burn to a crisp at high noon! In short, they informed the monk that he could make a federal case out of the incident. They advised him not to fritter his time away but go right to the district attorney's office in the big city and tell him that some Jews cheated him out of a ticket which had won 75,000 and wouldn't give it back to him. You get the picture? Well, the monk didn't waste time and did everything he had to do—even more than he had to. It was then that they impounded the ticket and, gradually, the hodge-podge grew. And it was no laughing matter, either. As if things weren't bad enough, another problem entered the picture, another snag—a monk! Wanting to settle, my brother offered him ten, then fifteen thousand, but the monk turned a deaf ear to him. That monk was so dazed, he himself didn't know what he wanted. And that's the story of the snag. You get the picture?

Well then, where was I? Oh, yes, the snag. We couldn't do a thing with this heaven-sent snag. Couldn't turn left, couldn't turn right. But there's a great God up above who, like they say, punishes with one stroke and heals with the other. So, we found some people, buddies and pals, brothers-in-arms, do-gooders, and just plain hangers-on who stepped into the midst of the affair and tried to make peace. They finagled here and there, they ran from party to party—from my brother Henikh to the monk, from the monk to my brother, from me to Birnbaum, from Birnbaum to me, from both of us to my brother, and from all three of us to the monk. We hustled and bustled, traveled and argued. In brief, after much difficulty, they finally smoothed things over. Don't ask *what* or *how* they smoothed over. So long as things were smooth. Like they say: you stew up your troubles and eat a hearty meal.

Or as my brother put it when he met the monk.

"Your grace, this isn't the greatest decision in the world, but let's split it down the line."

"All right, we'll split it. But you're still a swindler, Henikh."

"I drink to your health, father," said my brother offering him a glass of whisky. We all drank buttoms-up, kissed each other. Everything was fine and dandy. Everyone was satisfied. Satisfied? How could *anyone* be satisfied if each of us practically had 75,000 in our grip and had let it slip away. Blast it! You want to know how it happened? Here are the plain facts. I'm not even going to talk about myself. So what if I don't have the 75,000! I don't give a damn. But I ask you, what would my brother Henikh have done if I hadn't wired him about our 75,000 ruble prize? Do you know what someone else in my shoes would have done, seeing such big money? He would have buttoned his lip and mum's the word. What brother? Who's Henikh? Let him think I sold the ticket outright. Or that I pawned it with Birnbaum and didn't buy it back in time. For doesn't Birnbaum have a receipt from me saying that I pawned ticket number such-and-such and if I don't buy it back in time then said ticket would be his? You get the picture? But the point is, I swear I never so much as thought of any fast deal like that! You're looking at a man who doesn't give a damn for money. When you get down to it, what *is* money? Dirt! Like my wife says, so long as you got your health and everything else you need. . . . But, then again, it was aggravating. After all, it was 75,000. You get the picture?

Now take Birnbaum, for instance. He's completely innocent. Poor chap, he let the 75,000 slip right through his fingers. Simply an honest and high-minded young man was he, who wanted absolutely no gain from a ticket not his own. He only wanted people to judge. To hear what others would say. You get the picture? For otherwise the situation would have been peaches and cream for him. After all, he had my note saying that if I didn't buy back the lottery ticket within a certain time, then that ticket numbered such-and-such would be . . . you get the picture? Well, as luck had it, that very ticket won the 75,000. Now, I ask you, isn't that enough to give you a fit? So much for two poor devils into whose pockets the 75,000 had almost come. Right?

The third poor devil was my brother, Henikh. He moped around like a dead chicken. It was *indeed* a pity that he was getting such a small share of the prize. After all, he was used to winning no less than 75,000 *every* year, *twice* a year, in fact! He went around yelling: "What do they want of me? Give to the monk, give to my brother, give to Birnbaum. They want to make a pauper out of me." You get the picture?

The fourth man, the monk that is, was certainly a poor devil. He swore, and you had to believe his word of honor, that he couldn't understand why the Jews were splitting up his money. "Henikh, at least, despite the fact that he's a swindler and deserves to be locked up, is, after all, a home-town friend. But the rest of the bunch? What sort of partners are they to my ticket?" You get the picture? Well, try and speak to a monk and explain the meaning of honesty—that one was a brother who could have taken the entire sum without anyone saying boo, and the other was such an honorable young man, who had my note which stated that lottery ticket number such-and-such . . . you get the picture? Did Birnbaum have any ill-intent? Did he demand anything? Did he have any complaints? God forbid! He only wanted to call in outsiders to judge. Whatever other people would say! He'd suddenly fallen in love with people. You get the picture?

Well then, four people each won a part of the 75,000 and each of them lost the full 75,000. Four ruined, unhappy souls. But having settled, there was no use crying over spilled milk. Perhaps it was fated. Well then, what was the next move? To go and share the prize—that is, all four of us would have to go to the bank, take the ticket, collect our money, divide it, and shout congratulations over a glass of wine. Right? Well, take it easy, hold your horses! First of all, the ticket had been impounded by the judge. So the first thing to be done was to liberate it. But the monk didn't want that done until his share of the prize was guaranteed. You get the picture? But how could his share be guaranteed? Only by taking it from the rich man's account and writing it over to Henikh and the monk. But the rich man didn't want to hear of it, and rightly so. Here's what he said:

"What do I care about someone else's ticket. How can I order the release of a 75,000 ruble ticket which isn't mine and which has been impounded, if I don't even know whose it is. First it belonged to Birnbaum and Yakov-Yosil. Now, the latest is that it belongs to a Henikh and a monk. Later, other owners will show up, other Henikhs and other monks. What will I do if each of them demands the 75,000 from me? Friends, where would I get all that cash? I'm not Brodsky, you know."

You get the picture? Then a run-around with lawyers started. And lawyers are just like doctors. Whatever one says, the other says just the opposite. But they all take money and give advice. Each of them, different advice. One lawyer said that the rich man could very well hand the ticket over to anyone he wished. Another said that he could not hand it over under *any* circumstances. A third comes to say that he *had* to release it, for, if not, he could get himself into hot water for *not* hand-ing it over. Then came another lawyer who said that the best thing would be for the rich man to wash his hands of the ticket altogether. Another lawyer said: mention it not! If he washed his hands of the ticket, the ticket would be left dangling in mid-air, and then he'd *really* be in hot water. Another lawyer said: just the opposite. If he *didn't* give up the ticket he'd be in hot water. Then a new lawyer showed up with a new idea: The rich man could either give it up or not—he'd have a pack of troubles in any case. You get the picture? But I think the rich man had himself a pack of troubles anyway. Aside from the fact that they kept annoying him every minute, he had to hustle into the big city every week, run from one lawyer to the next, pay their fees, and beg them to have pity and tell him how to get rid of that load of TNT he'd latched on to. It *was* a pity, I tell you, a downright shame! They took an honest, easy-going chap who wouldn't hurt a fly, hung a pack of trou-bles on his back, and told him to keep it. But what ever for? Why does he have to carry such a load of TNT? Because others wanted to make peace and do a man a good turn . . . you get the picture? Do you hap-pen to have another load of TNT—damn it—I mean another cigarette?

Well then, where was I? Oh yes, the TNT they hung on to our rich man's back. No doubt you want to know what happened to it. Nothing. The TNT was still TNT. It was still up in the air. Our rich man hopped back and forth to the big city, seeing the money-grabbing, advice-giving lawyers. This one said this, that one said that, and the third one said neither this nor that, but, as you'd expect, something entirely different. How it would end up, only God knew, for no human mind could con-ceive of the outcome. If, heaven forbid, it ended up in court, who knew what the result could be. You get the picture?

But, in the meantime, who was buried six feet under? Yakov-Yosil! I had dealings with the whole city—what am I saying, *city*? The whole world! Everyone pointed at me and said: "There goes the 75,000." I was cut off from business; I didn't have a kopek in my pocket; it was worse than before. My wife was ashamed to show her face at the market-place—they kept calling her, "the new Mrs. Well-to-do." At the syna-gogue, they honored me in an entirely new fashion. They figured out how much I'd have to contribute to the communal funds, how much to give my poor relatives, and what I'd do with what's left over. One said, I'd probably become a money-lender. Another suggested that I be-come a wheat-dealer again. A third proved that it would be best for me to open up a business office. That way I'd have the finest business in town, for which office in our town had a capital of 75,000? And they're speaking of cold, ready cash. You get the picture? For our village is made up of a mob of doubting Thomases. No one believes that there's a merchant in town who has twenty-five rubles he can call his own. I want you to know that our village is a right and proper one—it hasn't gone to the dogs yet. Not much! People look twice before they leap into things. There are plenty of loafers who, for lack of anything better to do, go from Shmerel to Berel and slander the whole world. They have no business of their own, so they mind everyone else's. They assemble in front of the marketplace drugstore known as the stock-exchange and they estimate everyone's worth. They quiver and quake if someone else is making money. They're pleased as punch if someone goes into the red. Now you can imagine what sort of blue funk the town fell into when they heard about the 75,000. They've been jabbering about it from dawn to dusk ever since. They exchange quips and thorny digs. They eat each other's hearts out and cut each other to the quick.

"Why didn't *you* win the 75,000 rubles? You could have well used them."

"Why didn't *you*? You need it more than *I* do!"

So as to vex them, one calculator figured out that I was the richest man in the village. Quite simple, he said. I'd won 75,000, he said, and my apartment was worth 6 or 7,000. That made a grand total of 85,000, nearly 100,000 rubles, he said. Then, after all, he thought, if a Jew says that he had 100,000 rubles, you could well depend on his having 200,000, for if he's valued at 200,000, the calculator said, he doesn't even have 100,000. In other words, I had 200,000, and was therefore the richest man in town. But if you ask: aren't there any men richer than me? I'll answer—how can we tell? Who has crept into their pockets or counted their cash? Who knows if they haven't come down in the world? You get the picture? This really rankled many people to the core. They just couldn't take it, poor souls. Why should a down-and-out Jew suddenly and out of the blue fall into 75,000, without lifting a finger?

There's a rich old miserly bachelor in our village. One day, our gang purposely sent Mendel the Beard over to his house to deliver the good news that Yakov-Yosil had won 75,000. He got so sick—may you be spared—that they thought his end had come. Tsk, tsk, what a pity! He stumbled around in a dither for days. But, after he heard about the snag and the incident with my brother Henikh, he fully recovered. "Better let the monk get the money," he said. "Why should a Jew get such a big sum?" You get the picture? I bet you think that at least those close to me don't begrudge me the money! But they're so riled they're liable to drown me in a teacup. Take my word for it, if the 75,000 would have been mine and mine alone, the picture would have been entirely different. Everyone would have gotten his share—relatives and friends alike. However, since things are the way they are—what can I do? But

never mind, the family can well start preparing big purses and see what
they can tap out of my brother. After all, Henikh is a big sport. When
he starts shelling out, the world will stand up and take notice. There's
a rumor that he's already earmarked a dowry of 72 to 75 rubles for his
poor unmarried sister. He's also given all of a hundred rubles to his
aged father. Let his old man know and realize that his son has won
75,000. You get the picture? So much for local relatives. As for far-off
kin . . . they just kept dropping in out of nowhere, each with his own
hard-luck story. Many of them had already started arranging matches
and weddings on account of the prize money. Some of them got di-
vorced so that they'd be able to remarry into richer circles. Well, at least
they're relatives. Like they say: suffer with your own. You get the picture? But complete strangers? Must I bear the brunt of *their* troubles?
Have I deserved a fate like that? What wrong have I done? I wish a
75,000 ruble prize on all my enemies. I swear that I can no longer
stand all those congratulations, those sweet fawning smiles and little
flatteries. People I've never before seen in my life come up to me and
ask my advice.

"We've heard about you, Reb Yakov-Yosil. We've known all along
what a wise man you are. Don't you think that this has anything to do
with the big prize with which God has blessed you. Heaven forbid. We
dropped in just like that to pour our hearts out to you."

You get the picture? One man even came from some queer town in
a distant land whose name I've forgotten and where my grandfather's
grandma had never been. One day, the door suddenly opens up and in
walks a Jew who puts his bundles on the floor.

"Hello."

"Hello yourself. Where you from?"

"From hunger! Are you Reb Yakov-Yosil?"

"That's me. What's the good word?"

"Are you really *the* Yakov-Yosil who won the 75,000? I purposely
came to see you. What I mean is, I was passing by anyway and I heard
that you'd won the 75,000, so I decided to drop in for a day. I wanted
to set my eyes on that lucky man who'd won 75,000. It's no trifle. After
all, it is 75,000!"

You get the picture? Go explain to each and everyone the details
about Birnbaum who wanted mediation, a brother named Henikh, the
snag in the proceedings, the rich man, the load of TNT, the lawyers, the
devils, the plagues! I swear, I was better off before the 75,000 than now,
after the 75,000. Certainly things were quieter. To tell you the truth,
I'm afraid for my life now! Just the other day, I was in the big city, seeing the lawyers. That night, I met up with some scoundrel who lured
me to his home in the downtown slums, supposedly for a cup of tea.

When I got there, I met another one of the gang, a decent-enough looking fellow with a long beard, sitting and studying. He greeted me, rose
to light a cigarette, but suddenly put out the light instead. All of us were
left in the dark. You get the picture? I swear, here's another story worth
telling, but it's quite late and you're in a rush to get home. Anyway, this
story is linked up with another one. Like they say: a pimple on a blister, a blister on a boil. You get the picture?

Well then, where was I? Oh, yes, at the end of the story. You think
that's the end of it? Hold your horses, take it easy! This is just the start.
What am I saying, *start*? The start hasn't even begun yet! And whose
fault is it? My very own! Then again, why mine? How do I know? After
all, I'm just a human being made out of flesh and blood, like they say.
And, if misfortune is fated, is there any getting around it? Why is it my
fault that I . . . but wait a minute. You're not supposed to put the horse
before the cart, I mean, the cart before the horse. Let me tell you the
whole story, not from the very beginning, but from the beginning of the
end. In any case, if you remember, after much worry and trouble, we
finally decided with the good Lord's help to share the winnings.
Naturally, this was easier said than done. There was plenty of yelling
and bickering among us. The monk argued—why are Birnbaum and I
getting a share? My brother Henikh was hell-bent upon me relying on
his honesty, good will, and sense of understanding. And my Birnbaum
shouted that he didn't want a thing—he only wanted people to mediate, to hear what others would say. You get the picture? Well then, some
brokers poked their noses in—three of them at once. They sweated
over it, straightened things out, and put an end to the affair. And, if you
remember, the upshot was . . . well what *was* it? We decided to get together, all four of us that is, and take a trip to the big city, secure release
of the ticket, pick up our bit of money, split it, and wish each other a
fond farewell. But all this was fine and dandy if you had a ticket. But
what if there was no ticket? Could one say there was no ticket? Actually,
there *was* a ticket, but do you remember *where* it was? Locked up in a
bank under another person's name, and, begging your pardon, it had
been impounded by the court to boot. Try and release a ticket like that!
Well what could we do? The first thing we'd have to do was put an end
to the affair. Once that happened, we'd see what was to be done next.
You get the picture? But who *could* put an end to it. The monk, naturally. But he said, if you remember, that he wanted a guarantee—that
the ticket should be written over to him—and then he'd see to it that
the affair was closed. You think he was right, right? Who, then, was supposed to hand over the ticket so that the affair could be ended? The
rich man, naturally. So we came to our rich man and asked him to sign
the ticket over to the monk and then the whole affair would be closed.

But, once again, our rich man rightly argued: "What do you want of me? Why latch another affair onto this one?"

"You're right," we said, "but what can we do if you're the only one who can put an end to this business."

"But is it my fault?" he said. "Put an end to the affair or not put an end to the affair. What affair is it of mine?"

You get the picture? Do you have an extra affair?—damn it—I mean, a cigarette?

Well then, where was I? Oh, yes, putting an end to the affair. We got advice here and there and finally decided to sue. Since it came to suing, we had to go to a lawyer. Since it came to a lawyer, we had to go to the big city. Then the question arose—which lawyer? One said to go to *this* lawyer, another said, *that* one. The outcome was, we had no choice and went to them both. What one lawyer said, the other, naturally, opposed. A third one pulled something entirely new out of his hat. We were in a bad fix, so we went to a fourth lawyer. In a word, do I have to tell you what sort of breed lawyers are? Lawyers and doctors are one and the same plague. Lawyers and doctors were created for the specific purpose of contradicting each other. Whatever one says, the other must say just the opposite. They're just like the Aramaic translation of the Bible. I have a friend who says that the Aramaic translator was a spiteful wretch. For instance, if the biblical Hebrew says: "And he said," the Aramaic says: "And he saith." And when the Bible says: "And he spoke," what harm is there, Mr. Translator, in saying: "And he spoke"? But no! The Aramaic says: "And he spake." Well, can you go fight him? You get the picture? One lawyer said that all four of us ought to serve notice against the bank and the rich man because they weren't giving us the ticket. Good idea—huh? Comes the other lawyer and says, only two of us, Birnbaum and myself, should serve notice on the rich man because he isn't asking the bank to hand the ticket over. That too seemed to be a good idea, right? But, then, the third lawyer said: what has Yakov-Yosil to do with the bank? Does the bank know him? Did it have any dealings with him? Let Birnbaum alone serve notice, not on the bank, but on the rich man. For is the bank at fault if Birnbaum himself had recently ordered transfer of the ticket from his to the rich man's account? Sounds logical, right? Then another lawyer came and said that neither I nor Birnbaum should serve notice. The monk and Henikh should serve notice. That made sense too, eh? Then another lawyer came and hit upon this plan. We should not sue at all. Let's take a look and see how the ticket came to be in the rich man's name. Birnbaum put it there. Where did he get it from? Me. Where did I get hold of it? From my brother, Henikh. Who did he get it from? He borrowed, I mean, bought it from the monk. Henikh said *bought*, the monk said *borrowed*. What difference did it make? It was a lost cause. In that case, let the monk demand it from my brother, my brother from me, me from Birnbaum, and Birnbaum from . . . from whom? Birnbaum from the bank. But the bank says that they don't know Birnbaum any longer—only the rich man. Then let Birnbaum demand it from the rich man and he from the bank. But the rich man was afraid of—of what?—of being sued. But there was another way out, said the lawyer. Birnbaum would sign a note and release the rich man, I'd release Birnbaum, my brother would release me, and the monk would release my brother. How's that for a brainstorm? Could there be anything better? Then another lawyer popped up and asked a silly question: Hold everything! How do we know that the trail of the ticket ends with the monk? Suppose there's another character hiding in a closet who's going to jump out tomorrow with a batch of witnesses and documents and claim: "The ticket's mine. Help! Where's my ticket?" What would happen then? He wouldn't demand the ticket, he'd demand the 75,000. Who from? None other than the rich man. But the rich man had a release note from Birnbaum, Birnbaum had one from me, I had one from my brother Henikh, and Henikh had one from the monk. The next step, the lawyer said, would be for the rich man to sue Birnbaum, Birnbaum me, I my brother, my brother the monk. Like the Passover song: *One Only Kid*—"the cat ate the kid, the dog ate the cat, the stick beat the dog, the fire burned the stick, the water put out the fire, the ox drank the water, the slaughterer killed the ox," and so on. You get the picture? Things were in a bad way again! What were we to do? We had to go to one of Russia's biggest lawyers, Kopernikov himself, and from him to the greatest lawyer of them all. In short, we didn't leave out a single one. We literally lawyered our heads off. Morning, noon, and night all we heard was lawyer, lawyer, lawyer. Do you happen to have a lawyer on you—damn it—I mean, a cigarette?

Well then, where was I? Oh yes, the lawyers. Finally, with the help of God, they hit upon a solution. After all—they are lawyers! What did they advise? Here's what they advised: Before we did anything else, I and Birnbaum, both of us that is, should sign a notarized statement saying that we two had absolutely nothing to do with the ticket; that we weren't parties to the affair at all; that the ticket was sent to me by brother Henikh who took, that is, bought it from the monk; and that Henikh asked me to pawn it which I did through Birnbaum for 200 rubles. In other words, the story as it really happened, the honest to goodness 100 per cent truth. When you get down to it, isn't the truth better than alibis, flim-flam, or makeshift excuses? But nobody thought of it before, you get the picture? But hold up, I'm not through yet. What did he mean by me and Birnbaum giving ourselves a slap in the face like that? What would become of our share in the prize money? What would happen later if the other two would say: kiss my—. Ought I depend on my brother's honesty and the monk's word of honor? But you'll say that we'd signed a paper and had drunk toasts. Nonsense! A piece of paper costs a kopek and toasts can be drunk every day, like they say, so long as there's a drop of whisky around. Then what did I and Birnbaum want? We just wanted a guarantee. We wanted our shares of the prize guaranteed. You get the picture? Here's where the picnic began.

"Guarantees!" they said. "Where do they come off deserving guarantees? It's enough they're getting money which doesn't belong to them. But guarantees?"

This touched us to the quick. "What do you mean? We deserve it for our honesty, you so and sos. It's enough that we're doing you a favor," we said. "We could have taken the whole 75,000 and no cock would have crowed. And you still complain?"

"In other words," they said, "we have to thank you and pinch your cheek, besides."

Those were Henikh's words. This got my goat! We exchanged tit for tat and had a row, as is customary among brothers. But—in a nutshell—things worked out. They would give us a guarantee. What sort? Receipts? A receipt is as strong as a thatched roof. Notes? They aren't worth the paper they're written on. What then? Cash? Like my grandma, may she rest in peace, used to say: "The best check is ready cash." But where would they get cash if in those days not a soul had any. What am I saying—not a soul? There *was* cash around, and lots of it, but the Brodskys had it.

"In short," I said, "it's all a lot of hot air. Until there's a guarantee, I'm not signing."

"What sort of guarantee?"

"Any kind at all, so long as it's a guarantee. I just don't want everyone to call me an ass later on."

You get the picture? That's number one. And my buddy, Birnbaum, took up his old battle-cry—mediation! Since he was about to sign over his part of the ticket permanently, he wanted to let other people judge. He would go by whatever they would say.

"Again people," I said. "I thought we dropped that. What good will they do you?"

"I want to hear what others will say, you understand," Birnbaum said. "Perhaps they'll find that I have nothing coming to me, then why should I take money for nothing?"

You get the picture? I'm screaming for a guarantee, and he's calling for mediation.

"We'll get the guarantee later," he said, "first let's see what other people will say!"

"You're on that people binge again, huh? You've got my head spinning with your people. Let's get a guarantee first. That's more important."

Well then, where was I? Oh, yes, the guarantee. Well, they gave us a guarantee, legally and properly connected each one of us to the other, and we all signed it at the notary's. The papers were presented at the right place and we again started going to lawyers, drawing up documents, documents of this and that sort, dashing into the big city every Monday and Thursday, paying good money to sleep in bedbug-ridden hotels (a plain inn wasn't good enough for them), dining on fried roaches, which the menu listed as roast beef (plain stew wasn't good enough for them), perspiring like in a Turkish bath, broiling in the sun, scuffing over the hot cobblestones, deafened by the city noises and dead-tired from the rush and the tumult. And for what? Big deal! 75,000! I wish the whole business would come to an end. Like my wife said, may she live and be well: "A bird in the hand is worth two in the bush. Your 75,000 has put 75 holes into my heart. And with due respect for all the glory—what do I need all this for?"

"Go on," I said, "you're a fishwife and you'll always be one."

But yet, I felt she was right. What good did that sum do me if I couldn't use it for shopping. All I did was breed unnecessary enemies. This one envied me, that one begrudged me the prize, afraid that I might get the money, for why should Yakov-Yosil come into such big money? You get the picture? It cost us plenty of health until we finally got the good word that the whole affair was over and done with. The whole affair was an affair no more. And you can imagine what a sight for sore eyes that ticket was. Think we got to see it so quickly? Hold your horses! Take it slowly! First, we had to wait a month in case anyone wanted to protest the settlement. I don't think I slept one night that month. I had such queer dreams. More than once—you get the picture?—I would wake up in the middle of the night yelling in a voice not my own: "Tsipora, I'm flying!"

"Where you flying to?" she said. "Flying all of a sudden! Spit three times and tell me your dream."

"I had a fine dream. I dreamed I had wings and was flying and was being followed by wild creatures—by flying serpents and dragons who wanted to kill me."

That happened once. The second time, I dreamed I was sitting on a sack, a huge inflated sack of red rubber which had "75,000" marked on it in large numbers. It was a summer Saturday and the whole town, men, women, and children, had gone out for an afternoon stroll. They all stopped and stared at me. Then—suddenly—BANG! There was a roar and my rubber sack burst. I felt myself falling, falling and screaming, "Tsipora, it burst."

"God be with you. Who? Who burst? May my enemies burst!" my wife said. Naturally, she thought the dream was all for the good, as a wife usually does.

Well then, where was I? Oh, yes, getting the ticket. When it came to taking the ticket out of the bank, something new came up. Who would participate? Everyone trusted himself to the core, but I wasn't obliged to rely on anyone *else's* honesty. It was too great a temptation. After all, it was 75,000 rubles. You get the picture? The upshot was—you didn't trust me—I don't trust you! Then let's all go together. What did that mean? It meant all ten of us. How come *ten*? Figure it out for yourself and you'll see. I'm one, Birnbaum is two, the monk is three, my brother Henikh is four, and three lawyers (the monk's, my brother's and the one representing Birnbaum and me). That makes a grand total of seven people—may no evil eye harm them. Then what about the three brokers who stuck their noses into the affair and brought us to terms? That makes an even ten. At first, it was a bit strange. My brother Henikh kicked up a storm about such a big mob coming. He thought that two would have been enough—he and the monk. He didn't at all like the idea that no one had faith in his honesty or the monk's word of honor. But it did him as much good as barking at the moon! Each one had a different and legitimate argument. For instance, I said that I *had* to go, for I was a brother. Not for dignity's sake, but because one brother would very well thumb his nose at the other. And what could I do to him then? Sue him? My own brother? My Birnbaum argued, if Henikh's own brother didn't trust him, why should he, a complete stranger, depend on miracles? He said that he'd done his duty. You couldn't say he was completely wrong either. There was no question about the three lawyers going. They *had* to be there, they said, for there would be plenty to legalize, notarize, and authorize. That left the brokers. The brokers claimed that they too had to come along and all three of them to boot. They were old hands at the game, they said; they were trained at the school of hard knocks; they'd gotten their experience at the Yehupetz stock exchange and knew what brokers' fees meant. Like the matchmaker's commission, it was the sort of fee that had to be paid on the spot. You get the picture?

We arranged to come, not all at once, but one by one. Since each of us anticipated being first, however, we all met at sunrise in front of the bank. We paced around for a long time until they opened the doors and let us in to take our ticket. I don't have to tell you what a bank is. A bank hates to rush—it takes its time. What did it care about a ticket, Yakov-Yosil, 75,000, monks, Henikhs, Birnbaums, the poor brokers who wanted a little commission, and the rest of the lookers-on? The bank didn't give a damn about it all. One smoked, another prattled nonsense, this one drank a glass of tea, that one sharpened a pencil, another read the paper. He had his nose buried in it and wouldn't have lifted it for all the tea in China. We walked around, yawned, coughed. We were on pins and needles, waiting for the big moment. But the bookkeeper still had not arrived. When he came, the cashier was still missing. When the cashier showed up, the director had yet to come. Where was he? Sleeping! In other words, the owner of the bank was still snoozing. After all, what did he care about tickets, Yakov-Yosil, 75,000, monks, Henikhs, Birnbaums, the poor brokers who wanted a little commission, and the rest of the lookers-on? How much did a director like him earn? I wondered. Six thousand for sure, maybe 8, and possibly all of 10,000 rubles. Why not? Poor chap overworked himself, didn't he? I swear, I would have taken his job for half the sum, a third of it, and I would have been more devoted and harder-working. That's what I thought at the time. On second thought, perhaps I didn't really think at all. You get the picture? Finally, the director came. As soon as he showed up, naturally, we all pounced on him at once. This evidently frightened him and he waved us away. The three lawyers and the monk went up to him and gave him the documents. You get the picture? The director locked himself up in his office with the papers and we had to wait and wait and wait. We waited until the moment we all waited for arrived. The director came out of his office accompanied by a fat aristocratic-looking gentleman. The director—begging your pardon—turned his backside to us and started an endless conversation with the blue-blood. What did he care about the ticket, Yakov-Yosil, 75,000, monks, Henikhs, Birnbaums, the poor brokers who wanted a little commission, and the rest of the lookers-on? Suddenly, the director turned around and said:

"Your papers are ready. Go to the cashier."

Now couldn't he have told us that at the beginning? With papers in hand, we dashed to the cashier, gave them to him, and thought that would be the end of it. But the upshot was, we hadn't even begun yet. The cashier was busy counting 100- and 500-ruble notes and had a table covered with piles of gold before him. How much money was there? Oh me, if I had a tenth of that—I'd laugh at the ticket. That's what I thought at the time. On second thought, perhaps I didn't really think at all. The cashier kept counting and didn't throw so much as a glance our way. What did he care about a ticket, Yakov-Yosil, 75,000, monks, Henikhs, Birnbaums, the poor brokers who wanted a little commission, and the rest of the lookers-on? The gold flew through his hands with a sweet tinkle. The music of gold! You get the picture?

Well then, where was I? Oh, yes, the gold. Having counted the gold, he pushed his glasses to his forehead and snatched the papers out of our hands. His fingers flipped expertly through them as if counting 100-ruble notes. He opened a drawer and removed a huge packet. From it he withdrew a large envelope. He ripped it open and took out *the* lottery ticket. "Who'll take it?" he asked. Ten pairs of hands shot out at him.

"Nothing doing," the cashier said. "I can't give the ticket to so many hands. Choose one of your group."

We then picked the oldest of the three lawyers. He slowly took the ticket with both hands, as if he were holding a baby about to be circumcised, and brought it first to the monk, then to my brother Henikh, then to me and Birnbaum, to both of us that is, to see if the ticket was the authentic one. The monk said he recognized it even while the cashier held it. He could tell by a certain sign. What the sign was—he wasn't saying. My brother Henikh swore that if, for instance, he were awakened at two in the morning and shown the ticket, he would immediately have recognized it. You get the picture? It so happened that I and Birnbaum *didn't* recognize the ticket. Why should I say something when I hadn't a leg to stand on? We carefully went over the series number and the number 12. Like they say: that's the main thing. Right? Then we immediately hurried over to the State Bank to cash our ticket and take that sweet bundle of 75,000. We all walked, although it was up-hill all the way. The oldest lawyer held the ticket over his head with two hands so as not to lose it and so that no one would suspect him, God forbid, of pulling a switch. You could never tell—it was such a jinxed ticket! You get the picture? We weren't ten now, we were more than twenty. Where did we pick up so many people—God bless them? I'll tell you. First of all, some good friends from my village just happened to be in the big city that day. Seeing that we were already on our way to the State Bank to pick up our 75,000, they decided to join us and watch the pay-off. For it wasn't every day that an event like that could be seen. In short—what a procession it was! At the State Bank, we were royally welcomed. Even the corporal who guarded the door was thrown for a loop when he saw so many Jews, and in their midst, a monk, swooping down at him. Nevertheless, he received us politely and admitted us into the bank, one by one. We saw those we had to see, said what we had to say, and were brought over to an official with a head as bald as a soup-bowl. They gave him the ticket and whispered something we couldn't hear. The baldy who sat at the other side of the latticed cage looked up, stared severely at us through his glasses, and continued working. He held a sharp little knife—you get the picture?—and scratched something into a notebook. He kept scratching and scratching. While he scratched, we stood there with our hearts in our mouths, watching him. The rest of the people watched us, inspecting us from head to toe. The bald official still kept scratching, and the rest of the clerks sat and counted money. Money wasn't the word for it! There was so much of it, it was like rubbish. Stacks of gold! It glittered before your eyes. The sight of it made your head whirl. Its tinkle made your ears buzz. Money, I wondered, who invented this thing which caused so much suffering and useless struggle. For money, one man was ready to swallow the next. Neither brother, sister, father, child, neighbor, friend, loved one existed—only money, money, money. Anyway, that's what I thought at the time. On second thought, perhaps I didn't really think at all. You get the picture? The official didn't stop scratching away. For what concern of his was the ticket, Yakov-Yosil, 75,000, monks, Henikhs, Birnbaums, the poor brokers who wanted a little commission, and the rest of the lookers-on? But there was a limit to everything. Finally, God took pity on us. The official stopped scratching, put his sharp little knife into his jacket pocket, took out a clean handkerchief, and royally blew his nose. Then he took the ticket, just as if it were a piece of scrap paper, opened a book, and started looking. First at the ticket, then at the book, then again at the ticket, and again at the book. This smartie probably thinks the ticket is a fake, I thought. Scratch and sniff away for all you're worth. The ticket is no fake, it's the real thing. Suddenly, I saw him take the ticket and practically throw it at our faces, saying (and I remember it word for word): "Who told you that this ticket won the 75,000?"

You get the picture? Who told us? Did you ever . . . ?

"What do you mean who told us?" we said. "The ticket itself told us we won the 75,000. Series 2289, number 12."

"Yes," he said, quite seriously, "that's true. Series 2289, number 12 *has* won the 75,000 rubles. But your ticket is series 2298, number 12. A slight error."

Well how do you like that? What can I say? When he first told us this we were all in a dither. We thought: either he's nuts, we're crazy, or perhaps it was all a dream. We looked at one another. Then, we finally remembered to have a look at the ticket. Yes, as we lived and breathed! Series 2298, number 12. You get the picture?

Well, my dear friend, what more can I say? I couldn't even describe a tenth of what happened, and you'd never be able to write it up. No one could possibly picture the scene which took place in the bank when we stood rooted, dumbstruck, looking at one another. Their faces were filled with—how shall I put it?—their faces weren't human any more—you get the picture? They were the faces of animals and beasts, beasts in human form. If looks could kill—there would have been wholesale murder that day. But so what? What was wrong? You've dreamed a dream of 75,000? Well, was it worth losing your life over it? Aside from money, wasn't life worth living? They were men completely crazy, you get the picture? But no one riled me so much as my buddy, Birnbaum. At least, the rest of the gang tried to make excuses and shift the blame on to the next fellow. The monk put the entire blame on my brother Henikh. Henikh said he didn't know a thing about the 75,000 and wouldn't have known a thing if it weren't for my congratulatory telegram. You get the picture?

"You certainly know how to read the paper, brother mine," Henikh said.

"Why didn't *you* look?" I asked.

"You were the big-shot," he said. "You had the ticket. You *owned* it."

Did you hear that? Before, when 75,000 rubles were involved, they wanted to cut me out altogether. Now that the dam had broken, I had become the real owner of the ticket. You get the picture? But never mind. I, Yakov-Yosil, who had always been the scapegoat, would take the entire blame. Fine, it's all my fault. But then, you asses, where were *your* eyes? You yourselves had seen all the papers and receipts and documents at least two dozen times, and there the series number 2298, number 12, was plainly written, while series number 2289, number 12, actually won the prize. Why didn't you think of looking and seeing that the 9 came before the 8? And when the ticket was in your hands, couldn't you have checked with the official list of winning numbers to see which series won the 75,000—series 2298 or 2289? You spared no effort in gathering up a mob and invading the bank. Why? Because you thought you'd be collecting. You get the picture? But Birnbaum burned me up most of all. You should have seen him standing there on the side like a complete stranger, as if the whole affair were no concern of his. A minute before, he'd been whipping up a storm. Mediation! Other people's judgment! And now he stood there, like a poor lamb, innocent as all get out. This cut me to the core and I decided to get even with him for the way he had tortured me that second of May, if you remember, when I stood and begged for the ticket like one before a thief.

"Mr. Birnbaum," I said, "now's the time to hear what people have to say. There are plenty of people here in the bank now—God bless them. Why so quiet? Don't you want to hear what others will say? You've given up on people, huh?"

The entire crowd stood there and had the time of their life. I can't tell you what they enjoyed more—me calling Birnbaum to the court of public opinion, or the kick they got out of the whole affair of 75,000 coming to naught. I can swear by anything under the sun that I don't give a damn for the money. Let it fry in hell for all I care. The only thing that bothers me is this: When they just *thought* I had 75,000, then Yakov-Yosil was known as Reb Yakov-Yosil. Now that it was known that Yakov-Yosil had beans and not 75,000, he was through. He was no longer Reb Yakov-Yosil. You leper-headed bastards! What sins did I commit? Yes 75,000, no 75,000. What difference did it make? Listen to me, Mr. Sholem Aleichem, you can sure be proud of your Jews and of the whole world! I tell you it's a lousy world. Phooey! It's a false and foolish world, a world led astray. But admit it—aren't your ears ringing and isn't your head spinning from my story of 75,000? Sorry that I've chewed your ears off. Live and be well—you get the picture?—and God grant us better business in days to come.

THE RUINED PASSOVER

"PARDON ME, REB Yisroel, but can you have the boy's new suit ready for Passover?"

That's what Mama shouted to the stone-deaf tailor at the top of her lungs. Yisroel, tall and long-faced, constantly kept cotton in his ears. He half-smiled and waved his hands, as if to say: Sure it'll be ready. Why not?

"In that case, please measure him. But only on condition the suit'll be finished in time for the holiday."

Yisroel looked at Mama, as if to say: What a queer woman. Isn't one promise enough? From his chest pocket, he withdrew a long, paper measuring-tape and a pair of English shears. He then began measuring me up and down and from side to side. Mama stood next to me, giving orders:

"Longer. Make it longer. Wider. Make it wider. For God's sake, don't make the pants too small. And I want the jacket to be pleated. Make it a few inches longer. That's it! I don't want the waist to be tight, God forbid. I want it to look nice and proper. More, more! Don't be stingy with the cloth . . . the boy is growing."

Yisroel the Tailor knew quite well that a boy grew, but he continued working without saying a word. After taking all my measurements, he nudged me, as if to say: You can go now. You're all finished. I very much wanted the jacket to have the fashionable pocket and slit in the back. But I didn't know who to turn to. Yisroel rolled up the tape with two fingers and stammered broken sentences to my mother:

"It's a hard season . . . just before the holiday . . . lots of mud in the streets . . . fish expensive . . . potatoes like gold . . . not an egg in sight . . . lots of work . . . new clothes ordered? . . . no . . . just patches. If the rich Reb Yehoshua Hersh orders his old coat turned inside out, times are pretty bad . . . Reb Yehoshua himself! These are some times, huh? You can't beat it."

But this didn't impress Mama too much. She interrupted him with:

"How much will the whole thing come to, Reb Yisroel?"

The dear Yisroel took a bone snuff-box out of his jacket pocket, poured some snuff into the hollow of his palm, slowly brought his hand up to his nose; and expertly sniffed it into his nostrils. Not a drop landed on his mustache. Then he waved his hand and said:

"Tsk, what's the difference? We won't quarrel about it. You know what I mean? Reb Yehoshua-Hersh. Turn an old coat inside out! Things are bad."

"Now don't forget what I asked you, Reb Yisroel. I don't want it tight or small. I want a pleat. And the waist—wide and roomy."

"How about a sl . . . ?" I started to say.

"Shh, let me finish," Mama said, and banged her elbow into my ribs. "Remember, now. Neither small nor tight. A roomy waist and a pleat. For God's sake, a pleat."

"How about a pocket?" I tried again.

"Will you shut up?" Mama said. "Did you ever see a boy like that, mixing in whenever grown-ups are talking?"

The deaf Yisroel took the package of cloth under his arm, rubbed two fingers over the *mezuza* on the doorpost and said:

"In other words, you really want it finished by Passover! Well, have a happy holiday."

2.

"Well, speaking of the devil, here's Reb Gedalye. I was about to send for you again."

Gedalye the Shoemaker was an ex-soldier. His front teeth were missing and his huge round beard was scraggly in the center. Gedalye was a jolly sort of man who moved with a little dancing gait as he spoke.

"Reb Gedalye," Mama said to him, "can you have a pair of shoes made for me by Passover?"

"So you want it without fail for Passover, eh?" He asked Mama. "It's downright amazing! Everyone wants the stuff for Passover. I've promised Khayele, Reb Motel's wife, two pairs of women's boots. One for her and one for her daughter. I have to make *them* up. Reb Shimele's Yosele ordered four pairs of shoes for Passover. I have to make those. Then there's a long-standing promise to Reb Avrohom's Feygele for a pair of women's boots. Neither storm nor earthquake will stop me—they'll have to be ready for Passover. Moyshe the tailor asked for a pair of tips—I can't refuse him. Zyama the Joiner's shoes need a pair of heels. There's no getting around it. Asne the widow's daughter latched herself on to me and begged in the name of God that . . ."

"Let's make it short and sweet," Mama interrupted. "In other words, you *won't* have it done by Passover? In that case I'll send for the other shoemaker."

"Why shouldn't I have them done?" he said, wriggling. "For you, I'll put off the rest of the work. Your shoes, with God's help, will *have* to be finished for Passover. And no excuses!"

Gedalye the Shoemaker pulled out a piece of blue paper, bent down on one knee and measured my foot.

"Make it a wee bit larger," said Mama, "a little more . . . more . . . don't be stingy with a slice of leather! That's it. It shouldn't squeeze his toes, God forbid."

"Squeeze his toes," Gedalye repeated.

"I want the best leather, Reb Gedalye. You understand. No rotten stuff."

"Rotten," said Reb Gedalye.

"And I want good soles on them. I don't want them to wear out quickly."

"Wear out."

"And I don't want the heels to fall off, God forbid."

"Fall off," Gedalye said.

"Now you can go to Hebrew school," Mama told me. "I hope you at least appreciate what we're doing for you. If only you'd want to study, you could make something of yourself. If not, what will become of you? Absolutely nothing. You'll be a dog-catcher."

I myself didn't know what would become of me. I didn't know if I'd become a somebody, a nobody, or a dog-catcher. All I knew was that at that moment I wanted the shoes to squeak. Boy, did I want squeaky shoes!

"Why are you standing there like a scarecrow?" said Mama. "Why don't you go to school? Go on! You're not going to get anything else."

Gedalye started to go, then turned around. "In other words, you definitely want it for Passover," he said. "Happy holiday!"

3.

Coming home from school, I stopped off at the tailor's to see about the slit and the pocket.

The dear Yisroel stood, jacketless in front of a huge table, wearing a broad pair of ritual fringes, immersed in his work. Draped around his neck were several long threads. Pins were stuck in his vest. He made chalk marks, snipped cloth and scratched his back with a bent middle finger, talking to himself as usual.

"Go make them pleats . . . they want it roomy . . . and nice . . . what from? . . . the air? . . . You can cut your fingers to the bone . . . you just about make . . ."

A few tailor's apprentices sat around the table sewing, singing a song, their skillful needles flying. One jaundiced-looking, freckle-faced boy with a bit of a sunken nose sang in a bell-like voice, sewing to the rhythm:

> Oh you're going,
> Oh you're going,
> and you're leaving me alo-o-ne . . .

The others answered with a little scream.

> I'll stab myself!
> I'll hang myself!
> I'll drown myself!
> I'll do myself some ha-a-a-rm!

"What do you want, little boy?" Yisroel asked.

"A slit," I said.

"What?" He bent his head down to me.

"A slit," I yelled into his ear.

"A slit?"

"A slit!"

"Where do you want the slit?"

"In the back."

"What do you want in the back?"

"A slit. And a pocket, too."

"What sort of a slit? What kind of pocket?" Basye, the tailor's wife, butted in. She was a tiny woman, who performed three jobs at once. She rocked the baby with her foot, darned a sock with her hands, and fussed and fumed with her mouth. "What the devil! Slits and pockets! Where do we have material for a pocket? Pockets he wants! Let his mother send cloth for pockets and he'll get them. There's a fine how-do-you-do! Pockets!"

I began to regret the whole business. I just hoped Mama wouldn't hear about it.

"In other words, you really want to have a slit?" Yisroel asked me and took out his little snuff box. "Go home, little boy, you'll have yourself a slit."

"And a pocket, too?" I asked, pulling a long, sad face.

"Go home, little boy," he said. "I'll see that you have everything."

Happy as can be, I whizzed over to the shoemaker's place to ask about the squeak in my shoes.

But Gedalye the Shoemaker wasn't in. His assistant, Karpe, sat at the bench working on a sole. Karpe was a healthy, broad-boned peasant lad with a pock-marked face, wearing a leather head-band to hold down his stiff, black hair.

"What do you want, boy?" he asked in Yiddish, then showed off his knowledge of a few Yiddish phrases.

"I have to see your boss, Reb Gedalye," I said in Russian.

"Boss gone to circumcision party. To get drink," he said in his halting Yiddish, and tapped his Adam's apple to make his point.

I sat down in a leather-covered bench opposite him and started a long discussion about leather, leather-goods, shoes, soles, nails, until I got to the subject of squeaks. He spoke Yiddish, I, Russian. When he didn't understand me, I talked with my hands.

"I'm talking your language, you ninny," I said. "I want you to tell me why a shoe squeaks."

"Better keep talking Yiddish," Karpe said. He licked the sole and scratched a mark into it with his black thumb-nail.

"Why does it speak?" I asked in Yiddish now. "What do you put into the shoes to make them squeak?"

"Oh, squeaks?" said Karpe. "Sugar makes them squeak."

"Is that all? Sugar? How come?"

"With sugar," Karpe explained, "it clomps-clomps, squeak-squeaks."

"Oh," I said. "The ground-up sugar probably crackles there. Don't you put anything else in?"

"A little whisky," Karpe said, "a little bit of whisky."

"Whisky? You mean vodka. Why vodka? I can see sugar making it squeak. But how come vodka? What's that good for?"

Karpe strained himself in Yiddish and finally made me understand the reason for it. Before you put the sugar into the shoes, he told me, you have to soak the soles in vodka, otherwise the sugar won't take.

"Now I get it," I said. "If there's no vodka, the sugar goes to waste. And if there's no sugar, there's no squeak. Like the Mishna says: 'If there's no food, there's no Torah.'"

I opened my purse and gave Karpe my entire fortune. All the money I'd collected for *Hanuka* and *Purim*. I bade him a friendly goodbye. Karpe slipped his big, black, tar-smeared hand into mine and rattled off a Yiddish ditty.

I ran home to grab a bite, then went back to school to brag about the new clothes and shoes that were being made for me. A jacket with a pocket and a slit in the back. And shoes which squeaked. Really squeaked!

4.

"Mama, school's out," I said, as I came running home from school a few days before Passover.

"Big deal! May you live to bring home better news," Mama said, completely in a dither prior to the holiday. She tied kerchiefs around both maids' heads, gave them brushes, brooms, and feather dusters. She herself had a kerchief on her head, and all three women cleaned and rubbed, washed and scrubbed, making everything kosher-for-Passover. I didn't know what to do with myself. No matter where I sat or stood or went—it was the wrong place.

"Get away from the Passover cupboard with your bready clothes," Mama screamed, as if I were lighting matches near gunpowder.

"Easy there! You're stepping on a Passover sack."

"Don't even look in that direction. That's where the Passover borscht is!"

I kept moving from one spot to another and got under everyone's feet. They slapped and pinched and smacked me.

"May your rabbi shrivel up! Couldn't he keep you in school one more day, so you wouldn't spin around here like a top? As if there isn't enough work to be done! In civilized homes the children sit in one place, they do. Can't you pick yourself up and do something—how about reviewing the Four Questions?"

"Mama," I said, "I know the Four Questions by heart."

"Big deal!" she said, "as if it didn't cost me plenty to get you to learn them."

I just about managed to survive until evening when Father went around the house, holding a candle, a wooden spoon, and a feather duster, looking for last signs of breadcrumbs which he himself had previously placed on the window sills.

Only twenty-four hours left, I thought. One day and one night. Then I'll have my new holiday clothes and be dressed like a prince. I'll have a new jacket with a pocket and a slit in the back. And my shoes will squeak!

"What's that squeaking I hear?" Mama would surely ask.

And I'd pretend not to know what's going on. Then there'd be the Passover ceremony, the Hagada, the Four Questions, the four cups of wine and the holiday goodies; *latkes*, dumplings, *kugels*. Thinking of these treats, my mouth started to water. I had hardly eaten a thing that day.

"Recite your bedtime prayer and go to sleep. There's no supper tonight. It's the eve of Passover."

I went to sleep and dreamed it was Passover. I arrived at the synagogue with my father . . . my new clothes crackle . . . my shoes squeak . . . Squeak, squeak. . . . "Who's *that*?" strangers ask. "That's Motel, Moyshe-Khayim's little boy." Suddenly, from out of nowhere, there appears a black, kinky-haired dog. With a growl, he attacks me, grabs hold of my jacket, and wants to run away. Frightened, Father stands rooted and shouts: "Beat it, scat!" The dog pays no attention and tugs at me from behind, just where the split and the pocket are. He rips half the jacket and begins to run. I run after him with all my might and lose a shoe. I stop in a mud puddle—one shoe on, one shoe off. I start yelling and crying: "Help, help!" Then I awoke and saw our maid, Beyle, standing next to me, pulling the quilt and tugging at my leg.

"Look at him. You can't wake him. Wake up, lazybones. Your mother told me to get you up. We have to get rid of the last of the leaven."

5.

Father threw the wooden spoon, the feather duster, and the remaining bread crumbs into the oven. The house was ready for Passover. The whole place was spotless and kosher. The table was set. The four cups smiled at me from afar. Before long, Passover would come. Soon I'd be dressed in my holiday clothes. But until the tailor and the shoemaker delivered my things, my mother made *me* kosher-for-Passover. She washed my hair and scrubbed my head with an egg and hot-water solution, and tore my hair out as she combed me. I writhed. She pinched and slapped me and hit me with her elbow.

"Will you stop squirming like a worm? Did you ever see a child who won't stand still? You do him a favor and he doesn't appreciate it."

I lived through the scrubbing ordeal, thank God, then sat waiting for my new clothes, watching my father who had just come from the bathhouse with wet earlocks. He sat studying the *Code of Law,* swaying back and forth, chanting with a Talmud melody:

"For bitter herbs we use horseradish. Since it is hard, the radish may be grated."

I looked at my father and thought: he's the most devout Jew in the world; ours is the most kosher Passover; no one would have finer clothes than I. But why weren't they here yet? What was wrong? Perhaps they weren't finished in time for Passover, God forbid. Of that, I didn't even want to think. How would I be able to set foot in the synagogue? What would my friends say? How would I be able to sit down at the table? May it never happen, I hoped. I wouldn't be able to stand it.

As I sat thinking these sad thoughts, the door opened and Yisroel the tailor came in with his handiwork. Joyfully, I jumped up, knocked the bench over, tripped, and nearly broke my neck. Mama ran in from the kitchen, holding a Passover ladle.

"Where'd that noise come from? Who fell? Oh, it's you, eh? may you not go straight to blazes! You're a devil, a demon, not a boy. Didn't you get banged up, God forbid? Good for you! Don't jump! Don't run! Walk like a human being!"

Then to Yisroel she said: "Well, you kept your word, Reb Yisroel. I was about to send for you."

Yisroel half-smiled and waved his hand, as if to say: That'd be something, as I live and breathe! Me not keep my word?

Mama put her ladle away and helped me into my new trousers. Then she put on my new set of ritual fringes which she herself had made for me in honor of Passover. Over that she put my jacket, happy that it was wide and roomy.

I put my hand behind my back. Thunderations! There was no hint of either a slit or a pocket. Everything was sewn smooth and proper.

"What sort of an animal is this?" Mama asked suddenly, and started turning me around.

Yisroel took out his snuff box, poured a bit of the tobacco onto his palm, and sniffed into his nose.

"What sort of an animal is this?" Mama repeated, and spun me around again.

"Where do you see an animal?" Yisroel asked, and turned me the other way. "That's the pleat you wanted. You asked for a pleat. Did you forget about it?"

"Some pleat!" Mama said, and whirled me around once more. "What a botched-up job, blast it! Phoo! It's a shame. As I live and breathe, it's a shame!"

But this didn't faze Yisroel. God forbid! He looked me up and down like a professor and said that the suit fitted me perfectly. It couldn't be any better.

"Even Paris can't beat this work. It sings, as I live and breathe, the jacket literally sings."

"What do you say to the way it sings?" said Mama, bringing me over to Father. "What do you say to this song?"

Father spun me around, looked at the jacket, and concluded that the *trousers* were a bit too long.

Yisroel took out his snuff box and offered my father some snuff.

"The trousers *are* a bit longish, Reb Yisroel."

"What's that? Longish? Don't you know what to do? Roll up the cuffs!"

"Perhaps you're right," my father said. "But what do you do if they're too wide. If they look like two sacks?"

"Some fault! It's like saying—the bride's too beautiful," said Reb Yisroel, taking a pinch of snuff. "Wide, you say? Too tight is a thousand times worse."

I didn't stop feeling the back of the jacket. I kept looking for the slit and the pocket.

"What are you looking for back there?" said Mama. "Yesterday's snow?"

That old liar, I thought, and looked at Yisroel as if he were a thief. "You deaf ass! To the blazes with you and your daddy!"

"Wear it well," the deaf Yisroel told me, reckoning the cost of the work. Then, Father again took up the *Code of Law* and continued chanting: "He who has forgotten to eat the last piece of matzoh . . ."

"Wear it well," said Mama, after Yisroel had gone. She couldn't stop looking at the jacket. "Just don't start any of your shenanigans. Don't get into fights with the peasant boys and then with the help of God you'll wear it and wear it in good health."

6.

"Well, speaking of the devil, here comes Reb Gedalye," said Mama. "Are the boy's shoes finished?"

"And how!" he said with his little dance-like gait, carrying the shoes with two fingers, as if carrying a metal hoop of live fish, fresh out of the lake. "It's downright amazing! Everyone and his brother wants them for Passover. I worked myself to the bone, slaved away at shoes instead of sleeping. Once I give my word, I don't care if the world comes to an end."

Mama then put the shoes on me, squeezing and feeling the leather, asking if it pinched me anywhere at all?

"Pinch?" Gedalye said, "I think that another pair of feet could fit into those shoes."

"Stand up and we'll see," said Mama.

I stood and bent the sole, listening for the squeak. But where? what? when? Not a peep came out of them.

"What are you bending the soles for?" said Mama. "Take your time, the year's plenty long. I'll bet that you'll have them ripped, God willing, by next Passover. Now take a walk over to Yekhiel the Hatter and they'll get you a hat for the holiday. But be careful with the shoes. Step lightly on the soles. They're not made of iron."

We walked through the courtyard to Yekhiel's shop, which was right next door. Yekhiel was born white, hair and all, but since he always worked with hats dyed black, he was always smeared with soot. Both sides of his nose were always blue and his fingers black as ink.

"Well, hello, look what the cat dragged in," Yekhiel said, good-humoredly. "Do you want the hat for yourself, or for your boy?"

"For my son," said Father with pride. "But show me something proper . . . something . . . you know what I mean?"

"For instance?" Yekhiel said, looking over the hat-filled shelves.

"For instance," Father said, sticking out his fingers. "I want it to be nice and fine and good and cheap and . . . you know what I mean?"

"I have just the thing you're looking for," said Yekhiel, taking some hats down from the shelf. As he fetched each hat, it twisted and spun on its way down, as if by magic. He put one hat after another on my head, moved away, looked at my face, and said, smiling: "May God bless us! What a perfect fit! Well, how do you like that hat? That's some hat, eh?"

"No, Reb Yekhiel, that's not what I had in mind," said Father, sticking out his fingers again. "I want the hat to be Jewish, you know what I mean, yet stylish, without any fancy doodads. It should be proper and . . . and . . . you know what I mean?"

"Well, why didn't you say so?" said Yekhiel, using a long pole to bring down a hat from the topmost shelf. It was sort of oval, soft-brimmed, and full of checked colors. He held it on one finger and spun it quickly, like a windmill. Carefully, as if my head were made of glass and he were afraid of breaking it, he put it on the tip of my head. The hat barely touched my head. He congratulated himself and wished himself a year of bliss. On his word of honor, it was the only one of its kind in the store. Father bargained a long time for it. Yekhiel vowed that he was selling it so cheaply only for us. Practically below cost, he swore, wishing himself a kosher Passover and lots of health.

I saw that the hat was to Father's liking, for he stepped back and kept looking at it and smoothing down my earlocks.

"I hope it lasts through the summer, at least," said Father.

"Two summers," Yekhiel said, sidling up to him. "Three summers! As I live and breathe, that's some hat. Wear it well!"

By the time I got home, the hat had flopped over my ears. It was a bit too big, I felt.

"It's no tragedy. So long as it isn't too tight," said Mama, pulling the hat over my nose. "Just don't keep taking it off and putting it on. Don't touch it. Wear it well."

7.

When Father and I came into the synagogue, all my friends were already there: Itsik and Berel, Leybl and Ayzik, Tsodik and Velvel, Shmaye and Kopel, Meyerl and Khayim-Sholem, Shakhne and Shepsl. All were dressed in their holiday best. All wore new jackets, new shoes, new hats. But no one wore such an old-fashioned, long jacket with a pleat as I did. No one wore the kind of shoes I wore. And no one's hat was as queer as mine. I'm not even talking about slits and squeaks. They sure fooled me. They sure made a clown out of me!

The gang greeted me with laughter.

"Oh! So these are the clothes you bragged about? Where's the slit in the back, huh? Where's the pocket you mentioned? Why don't we hear the squeak in your shoes?"

As if I wasn't feeling blue enough, they rubbed salt into my wounds. Everyone threw another dig my way:

ITSIK: What sort of jerket is that you got?

BEREL: That's no jerket, that's a junket.

LEYBL: It's a smock.

AYZIK: It's a dress.

TSODIK: A petticoat!

VELVEL: And look at those pants. They're looney.

SHMAYE: Pantalooney!

KOPEL: A pair of long-johns with leather clompers.

MEYERL: And that hut of a hat.

KHAYIM-SHOLEM: A stove-pipe.

SHAKHNE: A noodle-pot.

SHEPSL: A slop-pail.

I was so boiling mad, I couldn't even hear the fine praying of Hersh-Ber the Cantor. Only when the congregation was wishing one another "Happy Holiday," did I finally recover. I returned with Father, heavy-hearted and depressed. I just about managed to drag my legs home. A fire burned within me. I couldn't enjoy a thing. Neither the four cups of wine, the Four Questions, the Hagada we'd read, the delicious peppered fish we'd eat with sauce-soaked matzoh, the hot dumplings and *latkes*, nor the rest of the tasty dishes. None of it meant a thing to me. Nothing attracted me. It all disgusted me. Everything was spoiled, ruined. . . .

At the table, Father, the king, sat dressed in a white linen robe, wearing his satin hat, reclining in his pillowed easy-chair. Mama, the queen, sat next to him, wearing her splendid wedding-dress, a silk kerchief, and a necklace of beautiful pearls which made her so charming. I, the prince, sat opposite them, outfitted from head to toe in brand-new clothes. To my left sat Beyle the maid, wearing a new calico dress and a white, starched apron, which crackled and rustled like a matzoh. To my right sat Breyne, the mustached cook, her hair covered with a new yellow kerchief. She held her head with one hand and swayed back and forth, all set to listen to the Hagada.

"This bread of affliction," sang the king in a fine voice, as the queen, her face shining like a star, helped him lift the plate with the matzohs.

Beyle lowered her red hands to her apron, which rattled like a newspaper. No sooner did Breyne hear something in Hebrew, than she pulled a religious face and contorted her features, ready to have a good cry. Everyone was in high spirits; everyone was in a holiday mood. But the prince wasn't in step with the rest of them. His heart had turned to stone. A mist came over his eyes. Were it not for the Passover feast, he would have begun to weep. A spell of crying, perhaps, would have done him good.

"This year we are slaves, but next year we shall be free men," the king sang proudly and sat, making himself comfortable in the pillowed easy-chair.

Then, everyone sat, waiting for the prince to rise and ask the Four Questions: "Wherefore is this night different from all other nights?" —to which the king would answer: "We were slaves for Pharaoh in Egypt. . . ." But the prince sat as if he were tacked to the chair. He couldn't budge.

"Well?" the king motioned to him.

"Get up," said the queen. "Ask your father the Four Questions."

The prince didn't move. He felt as if someone had taken him by the throat with a pair of tongs and was throttling the life out of him. He bent his head to a side. He felt his eyes popping from their sockets. Two round pearl-like tears trickled from his eyes, rolled down his cheeks, and fell on the Hagada.

"What is it? Why the tears all of a sudden in the middle of Passover service?" the queen yelled in a rage. "Is that your thanks for the new clothes we made you for the holiday?"

The prince wanted to stop crying, but couldn't. The tears pinched and choked him. Suddenly an entire fountain, a well-spring of tears opened up.

"Tell us, what is it? What hurts you? Speak up. Answer! Or do you want Father to lay you down and give you a sound thrashing in honor of Passover?"

The prince stood up and stuttered:

"Question! I want to ask you four fathers . . . I mean, father . . . I want to ask you four que . . . que . . . que . . ."

The prince's legs buckled under him and he fell, his head on the white tablecloth, crying and sniffling like a baby.

A ruined . . . a completely ruined . . . Passover!

FROM THE RIVIERA

DON'T ASK ME what the Riviera is. I *used* to be in the dark about it and I hope you *remain* that way. I wish *I* never got to know it. So you want to know all about the Riviera in a nutshell, huh? In three short words it's: Jew-boy give cash! Riviera—that's a spot in Italy dreamed up by the doctors in order to wring the public dry. The sky there is always clear. We have the same sky here. Same sun, too. But the sea bothers the day-lights out of you. It rears and roars; it makes your head spin. But you keep paying. For what? For nothing at all. Absolutely nothing. Because you're an ass and have let yourself be hoodwinked into the Riviera— shell out! And you certainly do!

Just try and outsmart them, try not to pay! Do you think they argue with you? Insult you? Embarrass you? God forbid! They're as good as gold to you. They kill you with kindness. But the Riviera has one good point—and there's no denying it—it surely is warm there. Wherever it's warm, folks say, you don't cough as much. And there it is warm all year round, winter and summer.

Does it make sense? Surely it makes sense. If the sun shines—it's warm. But what of it! If it gets hot enough, our village is no icebox ei-ther. So, they come back at you with—fresh air! True, the air isn't bad there. Smells quite good, in fact. Like perfume. But it's not the *air*, re-ally. It's the oranges they grow. Then again, is it worth going all the way out there just for that? I don't know! There's plenty of air all over, I think. And oranges can be bought here, too. But the doctors say there's no comparing one type air with another. Perfumed air can cure. That's what the doctors say. But who cares what doctors say. Go listen to doc-tors! Why do they tell you that the Mediterranean soaks every sickness out of you? I don't deny it. Perhaps it is a sickness-soaker. All *I* know is that it soaked every last kopek out of me—that sea. And not so much the sea as those doctors. God sent a doctor my way, there at the Riviera . . . how should I put it? He was some doctor! That is, he was quite a likable fellow, otherwise. A Jew, to boot. And what a Jew! He spoke

Yiddish just like you and me. And what a juicy, spicy, free-and-easy
Yiddish, too. It was a pleasure listening to him. But the way he took you
for a ride! Boy, could he take you for a ride! And you know, I'm just the
sort to be taken. He certainly found the right customer. I made up my
mind—you hear?—and let myself be led by the nose right up to the last
minute. I saw right off who I was dealing with. But I played dumb. You
want to soak me. Go ahead and soak me.

First off he sounded me out, examined me, tapped me with little
hammers and bangers, tubes and pipes, and told me to come the next
day. I said to him: "Pardon me, doctor, but I'm not familiar with the
local procedure. How much do I owe you?" He looked at me through
his glasses, his hands in his pockets, and said: "We'll get to that later."
Fine, I thought. Later is fine with me. When I came the next day, we
went through the same rigamarole. He examined me, sounded me out,
pinched and hammered me. Then he told me to come the next day
and get an injection.

"Pardon me, doctor," I asked him. "How much do I owe you?"

"Later," he said.

Wonderful! Later was fine. The next day, he gave me a shot and told
me to come the following day for a massage. I came for the massage
and he massaged me, that is, he rubbed the spot where I'd been in-
jected and told me to come the next day for another shot.

"How much do I owe you?" I asked.

"Later," he said.

Fine. I didn't care. And that's the way it went, from day to day. One
day he gave me a shot, the next day he massaged the sore spot. That
swindle didn't appeal to me from the start. You want to get me coming
and going, eh? Well, go right ahead. But why make it a slap-down,
dragged-out affair? Who said you need one day for a shot and another
one for the massage? It seems to me that both operations done in one
day would be better. It's logical. Inject and rub it in at the same time.
But what's the point? Procedure? Of course not! Then I had to assume
that he wanted to milk me dry. Well, try it! Perhaps I'm not milkable.
Perhaps there's nothing to milk from? Do you know me? Did you ever
look into my pockets? Have you counted my cash?

Well, here's what happened. A month later, he mailed me a bill. As
soon as I looked at it I saw stars. Each injection cost 10 francs (there
they soak you in francs), and each massage cost five. Not a bad little
bill, eh? Cures like that can make a rich man out of you. What should
I do? I thought. Bargain with him? That I could always do later. If that
wise-guy didn't demand his money, why should I rush? So I kept getting his injections every other day. I come—he injects. The winter
came and went. Before I knew it, Purim had arrived. Time to start

thinking of the trip back home. Especially since my health, thank God, was good—quite good. In fact, I can well say—and why deny it?—I hope it never gets any worse. Of course, better has no limits. In that case, I had to say goodbye to that smartie of a doctor and go home. When I saw him, I said: "I'm going home."

"Have a nice trip," he said.

"Well, what about the bill?" I said. "I have to pay you off, don't I?"

He looked at me through his glasses, his hands in his pockets, as if to say: What's keeping you from paying?

"I hope you'll pardon me, doctor," I said, "but before we settle the account, I'd like to tell you a story, if you can spare the time."

"I really don't have the time to spare, but if it's short, tell it."

I sat down and told him the following tale:

"Looking at me, you can see I'm an average Jew. Thank heaven, I also have five boys, God bless them. Four of them happen to be fine and talented. But one of them—may you be spared a like fate—is the devil-knows-what! Didn't want to study—not a bit. A bad boy. We slapped him, beat him, but we couldn't knock the mule out of him. Neither kindness nor threats helped. A bad boy. Well, what was I to do?

"Put him into apprenticeship," my wife suggested.

"What? You want him to be *worker*? Over my dead body!"

"What then? What'll you gain if you beat him to death?" she said.

I considered it and decided she was right. I made a deal and turned him over to the best tailor in town.

"Take this prize-package," I said, "and make a workman out of him."

I signed a contract with the tailor. By the end of three years, he would have to make a tailor of my son and I would pay the master-tailor three hundred rubles. After the first year, he came around, took the first hundred, and signed for it. Wonderful! Another year passed by. The tailor returned, took the second hundred, signed for it. Fine and dandy. The third year passed by—but my tailor didn't show up. I waited a week, then two. Nothing! What had happened? I took a walk over to the tailor's place.

"Mr. Tailor," I said, "why haven't you come for the third hundred?"

"You don't owe it to me," he said.

"It doesn't make sense," I said.

"It makes plenty of sense! Three things make a tailor. First of all, he must know the work itself. Second of all, he must know how to make off with a piece of left-over material. If you want to call it robbery—go right ahead. Call it what you will. Third of all, a tailor must know how to drink, that is, celebrate a festival with a few drops. Your son, then, is two-thirds of a tailor. When it comes to thievery, he's quite handy. When it comes to liquor, he can hold his own with the best of souses.

But a tailor he is not, and never will be. Therefore, why take the third hundred?"

After listening to this story, the doctor asked: "Well, what's your point?"

"My point is," I said, "that your work, like any other work, consists of three things. First of all, you have to be a good doctor. Second of all, you have to be honest. Third of all, a doctor has to know how to make money. Which of the first two points is outstanding on your part, I don't know. But as I live and breathe, you surely know how to present a bill. Now, let's dicker over the price. . . ."

May a plague wrack my enemies for every ruble I bargained off the bill. I ended up paying less than a *third* of it. But the cure wasn't even worth *that* much. For had I stayed at home and done nothing, and were I destined to get better—I would have gotten better *anyway*. So what good's the Riviera?

About the Translator

Curt Leviant is the author/editor of 25 books, including translations from the Yiddish of five Sholom Aleichem collections, four novels by Chaim Grade, and anthologies of short fiction by Avraham Reisen and Lamed Shapiro. His most recent translation is a memoir by Isaac Bashevis Singer, *More Stories from My Father's Court*.

Mr. Leviant is also the author of four critically acclaimed novels, *The Yemenite Girl*, *Passion in the Desert*, *The Man Who Thought He Was Messiah*, and *Partita in Venice*, works that have been praised by two Nobel Laureates, Saul Bellow and Elie Wiesel.

Curt Leviant has won the Wallant Prize and literary fellowships from the National Endowment for the Arts, the Rockefeller Foundation, and the Jerusalem Foundation. His stories have appeared in many magazines and been included in *Best American Short Stories* and *Prize Stories: The O. Henry Awards*. A new novel, *Diary of an Adulterous Woman*, will be published in Fall 2000.

DOVER·THRIFT·EDITIONS

FICTION

Six Great Sherlock Holmes Stories, Sir Arthur Conan Doyle. 112pp. 27055-6 $1.00

Silas Marner, George Eliot. 160pp. 29246-0 $1.50

This Side of Paradise, F. Scott Fitzgerald. 208pp. 28999-0 $2.00

"The Diamond as Big as the Ritz" and Other Stories, F. Scott Fitzgerald. 29991-0 $2.00

The Revolt of "Mother" and Other Stories, Mary E. Wilkins Freeman. 128pp. 40428-5 $1.50

Madame Bovary, Gustave Flaubert. 256pp. 29257-6 $2.00

Where Angels Fear to Tread, E. M. Forster. 128pp. (Available in U.S. only.) 27791-7 $1.50

A Room with a View, E. M. Forster. 176pp. (Available in U.S. only.) 28467-0 $2.00

The Immoralist, André Gide. 112pp. (Available in U.S. only.) 29237-1 $1.50

"The Yellow Wallpaper" and Other Stories, Charlotte Perkins Gilman. 80pp. 29857-4 $1.00

Herland, Charlotte Perkins Gilman. 128pp. 40429-3 $1.50

The Overcoat and Other Stories, Nikolai Gogol. 112pp. 27057-2 $1.50

Great Ghost Stories, John Grafton (ed.). 112pp. 27270-2 $1.00

Detection by Gaslight, Douglas G. Greene (ed.). 272pp. 29928-7 $2.00

The Mabinogion, Lady Charlotte E. Guest. 192pp. 29541-9 $2.00

"The Fiddler of the Reels" and Other Short Stories, Thomas Hardy. 80pp. 29960-0 $1.50

The Luck of Roaring Camp and Other Stories, Bret Harte. 96pp. 27271-0 $1.00

The Scarlet Letter, Nathaniel Hawthorne. 192pp. 28048-9 $2.00

Young Goodman Brown and Other Stories, Nathaniel Hawthorne. 128pp. 27060-2 $1.00

The Gift of the Magi and Other Short Stories, O. Henry. 96pp. 27061-0 $1.00

The Nutcracker and the Golden Pot, E. T. A. Hoffmann. 128pp. 27806-9 $1.00

The Beast in the Jungle and Other Stories, Henry James. 128pp. 27552-3 $1.50

Daisy Miller, Henry James. 64pp. 28773-4 $1.00

The Turn of the Screw, Henry James. 96pp. 26684-2 $1.00

Washington Square, Henry James. 176pp. 40431-5 $2.00

The Country of the Pointed Firs, Sarah Orne Jewett. 96pp. 28196-5 $1.00

The Autobiography of an Ex-Colored Man, James Weldon Johnson. 112pp. 28512-X $1.00

Dubliners, James Joyce. 160pp. 26870-5 $1.00

A Portrait of the Artist as a Young Man, James Joyce. 192pp. 28050-0 $2.00

The Metamorphosis and Other Stories, Franz Kafka. 96pp. 29030-1 $1.50

The Man Who Would Be King and Other Stories, Rudyard Kipling. 128pp. 28051-9 $1.50

You Know Me Al, Ring Lardner. 128pp. 28513-8 $1.50

Selected Short Stories, D. H. Lawrence. 128pp. 27794-1 $1.50

Green Tea and Other Ghost Stories, J. Sheridan LeFanu. 96pp. 27795-X $1.50

Short Stories, Theodore Dreiser. 112pp. 28215-5 $1.50

The Call of the Wild, Jack London. 64pp. 26472-6 $1.00

Five Great Short Stories, Jack London. 96pp. 27063-7 $1.00

White Fang, Jack London. 160pp. 26968-X $1.00

Death in Venice, Thomas Mann. 96pp. (Available in U.S. only.) 28714-9 $1.00

In a German Pension: 13 Stories, Katherine Mansfield. 112pp. 28719-X $1.50

The Moon and Sixpence, W. Somerset Maugham. 176pp. (Available in U.S. only.) 28731-9 $2.00

DOVER · THRIFT · EDITIONS

FICTION

THE NECKLACE AND OTHER SHORT STORIES, Guy de Maupassant. 128pp. 27064-5 $1.00

BARTLEBY AND BENITO CERENO, Herman Melville. 112pp. 26473-4 $1.00

THE OIL JAR AND OTHER STORIES, Luigi Pirandello. 96pp. 28459-X $1.00

THE GOLD-BUG AND OTHER TALES, Edgar Allan Poe. 128pp. 26875-6 $1.00

TALES OF TERROR AND DETECTION, Edgar Allan Poe. 96pp. 28744-0 $1.00

THE QUEEN OF SPADES AND OTHER STORIES, Alexander Pushkin. 128pp. 28054-3 $1.50

SREDNI VASHTAR AND OTHER STORIES, Saki (H. H. Munro). 96pp. 28521-9 $1.00

THE STORY OF AN AFRICAN FARM, Olive Schreiner. 256pp. 40165-0 $2.00

FRANKENSTEIN, Mary Shelley. 176pp. 28211-2 $1.00

THREE LIVES, Gertrude Stein. 176pp. (Available in U.S. only.) 28059-4 $2.00

THE STRANGE CASE OF DR. JEKYLL AND MR. HYDE, Robert Louis Stevenson. 64pp. 26688-5 $1.00

TREASURE ISLAND, Robert Louis Stevenson. 160pp. 27559-0 $1.50

GULLIVER'S TRAVELS, Jonathan Swift. 240pp. 29273-8 $2.00

THE KREUTZER SONATA AND OTHER SHORT STORIES, Leo Tolstoy. 144pp. 27805-0 $1.50

THE WARDEN, Anthony Trollope. 176pp. 40076-X $2.00

FIRST LOVE AND DIARY OF A SUPERFLUOUS MAN, Ivan Turgenev. 96pp. 28775-0 $1.50

FATHERS AND SONS, Ivan Turgenev. 176pp. 40073-5 $2.00

ADVENTURES OF HUCKLEBERRY FINN, Mark Twain. 224pp. 28061-6 $2.00

THE ADVENTURES OF TOM SAWYER, Mark Twain. 192pp. 40077-8 $2.00

THE MYSTERIOUS STRANGER AND OTHER STORIES, Mark Twain. 128pp. 27069-6 $1.00

HUMOROUS STORIES AND SKETCHES, Mark Twain. 80pp. 29279-7 $1.00

CANDIDE, Voltaire (François-Marie Arouet). 112pp. 26689-3 $1.00

GREAT SHORT STORIES BY AMERICAN WOMEN, Candace Ward (ed.). 192pp. 28776-9 $2.00

"THE COUNTRY OF THE BLIND" AND OTHER SCIENCE-FICTION STORIES, H. G. Wells. 160pp. (Available in U.S. only.) 29569-9 $1.00

THE ISLAND OF DR. MOREAU, H. G. Wells. 112pp. (Available in U.S. only.) 29027-1 $1.50

THE INVISIBLE MAN, H. G. Wells. 112pp. (Available in U.S. only.) 27071-8 $1.00

THE TIME MACHINE, H. G. Wells. 80pp. (Available in U.S. only.) 28472-7 $1.00

THE WAR OF THE WORLDS, H. G. Wells. 160pp. (Available in U.S. only.) 29506-0 $1.00

ETHAN FROME, Edith Wharton. 96pp. 26690-7 $1.00

SHORT STORIES, Edith Wharton. 128pp. 28235-X $1.50

THE AGE OF INNOCENCE, Edith Wharton. 288pp. 29803-5 $2.00

THE PICTURE OF DORIAN GRAY, Oscar Wilde. 192pp. 27807-7 $1.50

JACOB'S ROOM, Virginia Woolf. 144pp. (Available in U.S. only.) 40109-X $1.50

MONDAY OR TUESDAY: Eight Stories, Virginia Woolf. 64pp. (Available in U.S. only.) 29453-6 $1.00

NONFICTION

POETICS, Aristotle. 64pp. 29577-X $1.00

NICOMACHEAN ETHICS, Aristotle. 256pp. 40096-4 $2.00

MEDITATIONS, Marcus Aurelius. 128pp. 29823-X $1.00

THE LAND OF LITTLE RAIN, Mary Austin. 96pp. 29037-9 $1.50

THE DEVIL'S DICTIONARY, Ambrose Bierce. 144pp. 27542-6 $1.00

THE ANALECTS, Confucius. 128pp. 28484-0 $2.00

CONFESSIONS OF AN ENGLISH OPIUM EATER, Thomas De Quincey. 80pp. 28742-4 $1.00

NARRATIVE OF THE LIFE OF FREDERICK DOUGLASS, Frederick Douglass. 96pp. 28499-9 $1.00